LISA SUZANNE

Waiting
GAME

BOOKS BY LISA SUZANNE

A LITTLE LIKE DESTINY SERIES
A Little Like Destiny (Book One)
Only Ever You (Book Two)
Clean Break (Book Three)

MY FAVORITE BAND STANDALONES
Take My Heart
The Benefits of Bad Decisions
Waking Up Married
Driving Me Crazy
It's Only Temporary
The Replacement War

Visit Lisa on Amazon for more titles

DEDICATION

To my 3Ms.

CHAPTER 1

"What the hell are you doing here?" Luke demands.

"I came to stop this wedding," she says. "You can't marry her."

"Why not?" Luke asks.

"Because we all know it's not real," Michelle says, her tone full of accusations. "You still have feelings for me. It's the only reason you'd go through with this. Luke, don't marry her."

My brows dip. It's the only reason he'd go through with this? What the hell is that supposed to mean? Does she think he's marrying me as a show to get her back?

She really is freaking delusional. More reasons why we need a paternity test. Luke needs hard evidence that he really is this baby's father.

Luke snorts before his eyes turn on his brother. "And I suppose you're the one responsible for calling her to let her know I'm getting married?" He doesn't even dignify her delusional words with a response.

"Does it matter *why* she showed up?" Jack asks.

Luke rolls his eyes. "What do you want, Michelle?"

"I want you, Luke. I've *always* wanted you. I'm carrying your baby. Don't marry some girl you hardly know," she says, and I can't help my own very un-bride-like snort.

"And what, marry you instead?" he asks derisively.

She glances at Jack before she turns back to Luke, and I can't help but wonder what that small look was all about.

"Yes," she says, and cue the hands on her stomach that's barely even showing. "I want you to be happy. I want you to find something real with someone who deserves you, and that's not her. This baby deserves his or her parents to be together, not for her dad to be with some random chick he just met."

Oh hell no, bitch. Did she just take a shot at *me*?

I'm about to put on my fighting gloves, and I even see Josh fume with anger at her words out of the corner of my eye when Luke steps in again. "Marrying Ellie is what will make me happy. I've fallen in love with her," he says, his eyes locking on mine. "Nothing you can say here will stop us."

Jack loops a protective arm around Michelle's shoulders. "What if I have something to say?"

Luke and I both regard Jack with wariness.

"It has come to my attention that this entire thing is a sham," Jack says. "Apparently they have some agreement for the next year."

Very few people aside from Luke and me know that, so the culprit is most likely Kaylee, depending what she thinks she heard last night.

That damn traitor.

Luke's eyes move to his sister, and when I glance over at him, he looks angry and a little sad. He trusted her. She was the *only* one he trusted in his entire family.

Kaylee stands up, her shoulders hitched up with apologies as she looks at Luke. "I had to do something after what I overheard last night."

"What did you overhear?" Carol asks.

"They were fighting," she says to her mom but also to the group as a whole, "and Ellie said something about how they have to live together for the next year and she'd rather do it on friendly terms than fighting." Kaylee looks back at Luke as all the blood drains from my face. She's tossing out these secret conversations in front of Michelle...one of the main people that pushed Luke into having this idea in the first place, along with her father—Luke's boss.

"I'm sorry. I just...this is all so fast, and I'm just trying to protect your heart." Kaylee's hand is on her chest, which makes me think she's being sincere. She was just looking out for her brother...but running to the other brother in a very intense sibling rivalry couldn't have been the answer.

Luke lets out a heavy breath. "Not that I need to explain myself to you, but what you think you heard..." he shakes his head and lets out a mirthless, slightly maniacal laugh. "I once told Ellie how the first year of marriage is the hardest. If we can make it through that on friendly terms, we can make it through anything. After what I went through last time, I firmly believe it's all about that first year. And that's all she was saying last night."

Kaylee looks like she wants to say more, to jump in with how many times she tried to stop me and how I may have admitted things that don't align with what Luke just said, but the look he gives her silences her.

"It's nice of you to try to protect my heart," he says to his sister, and then he looks at me. "But Ellie already owns it." His eyes burn into mine, and I can't help but think the words he's saying right now are the truth.

I wish with everything I am that they're true...but history tells me otherwise.

He pauses, his eyes on mine, and then he turns back to his sister. "But it's great to know where you stand." He takes my hands in his and turns back to Manny. "Can we continue now, please?"

"Of course, sir," Manny says.

"You can't just continue," Michelle spits from where she stands still in the middle of the aisle the two of us walked down to join hands and speak our vows. Her words sound like a child throwing a tantrum.

He turns and looks at her like she's a nuisance, a fly that won't stop buzzing around. He lets out another one of those maniacal little laughs. He's trying to hold his shit together in front of the daughter of his boss, but she's pushing him right to the line. I have to wonder why the hell he ever got involved with her in the first place.

"Why, exactly, can't I continue with my wedding?" Luke asks calmly.

"Because I came here to stop you. You can't just ignore me," Michelle says as if that explains everything. She sounds just like Jack—she came here to stop us, and she always gets her way.

Not this time, bitch.

He chuckles. "Oh, that's right," he says. He squeezes my hand as if to brace me for something. "Whatever you say here doesn't really matter."

Michelle looks confused.

Jack does, too.

In fact, everyone gathered here does...except Nicki.

"Why doesn't it matter?" Michelle asks.

"Well, you see, we had a feeling Jack would do something to try to stop me from actually being happy for once in my life, or the media would show up." He nods to Michelle, as if to imply she's the media since we both know she'll run right back to Savannah. She probably has a recording device planted somewhere on her as we speak. "Or any one of a hundred other things that could go wrong, and this is something we both really wanted...so we made it legal earlier today."

Boom! In your face, Michelle!

God, do I want to scream that out. I refrain.

Her face falls. "You...you two...you're..."

"Married," Luke finishes. His eyes move to mine again. "Ellie managed to do what you couldn't. You might be carrying my child, but she carries my heart. She holds it in her hands, and I count myself the luckiest man in the world that I found her when I did."

I smile at our secret about the night we really met, and he smiles back at our little inside joke. My smile hides the well of emotion inside me as I wonder whether those words are true. He says them so earnestly, and when his eyes are on mine the way they are now, I can't help but believe him. Something's been holding him back, but we're married now. Surely it's time for him to admit the truth.

"Now if you'll excuse us," he says to Michelle, "we have a ceremony to finish in front of our friends and family. We have to pose for photos for the media, and we have to finish the show, which is all this is since the ceremony earlier was the one that mattered. You're neither a friend nor family, so you can go now."

She sputters, and Jack draws her in a little closer. "You can stay as my date," he says to her, and I hate Jack even more. He's doing everything he can to look like he's the good guy, the savior, while Luke selfishly takes care of his own needs and leaves the girl he knocked up in the dust while he marries someone he barely knows.

I know that's not what this is, but to everyone outside of our innermost circle, that's how it'll look.

Luke's jaw clenches as Michelle looks over at Jack with hearts in her eyes. He doesn't say anything.

Luke just gives Jack and Michelle a look of disgust. "You two deserve each other." He glances at his brother. "Good luck with that train wreck." Then he turns back to Manny. "Can we continue now, please?"

Manny nods. "Join hands, and we will start over with the vows." Luke nods before he takes my hands in his and turns to me.

"Luke, do you take Ellie to be your lawfully wedded wife and equal partner, to join with her and share with her all that is to come, and to commit to a life together from now until you part?" Manny asks.

Luke nods as his lips tip up. "Yes, I do."

I can't help my own smile at his. Someone in the very small group of our guests makes a noise, but I drown it out as I lock my gaze on Luke and listen to Manny's words.

"And Ellie, do you take Luke to be your lawfully wedded husband and equal partner, to join with him and share with him all that is to come, and to commit to a life together from now until you part?" Manny asks.

"Yes, I do, too."

Luke's smile widens, and mine mirrors his. Maybe more noises come from the group, but I have no fucks left to give. This is between Luke and me.

"We will now exchange the rings." Manny nods to Josh, who hands over both our rings. Manny mumbles a few words over the rings then hands my set to him. "Luke, repeat after me as you slide the ring onto Ellie's finger. Ellie, I give you this ring as a symbol of our union. With this ring, I thee wed."

Luke repeats the words and squeezes my hand when he's done, and then it's my turn.

"Luke, I give you this ring as a symbol of our union. With this ring, I thee wed," I say, repeating Manny's words.

"You have consented to matrimony in front of the witnesses gathered here tonight. By the authority vested in me by the state of Hawaii, I now pronounce you husband and wife. Noho me ka hau'oli a mau loa," he says. "Live happily ever after. You may now kiss your bride."

Luke's mouth tips up in a soft smile that will imprint on my brain for the rest of time, and then he leans in and presses his lips to mine.

And fuck it all, we're putting on a show. I grab the back of his head and go for it.

I kiss him with all the pent-up passion I've reserved for my own private thoughts, and I don't even care that it's in front of these awful people who call themselves his family...plus my brother, Nicki, and my parents.

We haven't even opened our mouths to each other yet, but this is still the most passionate kiss I've ever experienced. Maybe it's because I'm pouring my soul into it just for him...and maybe he's pouring his in right back. It sure feels like it.

I'm about to open my mouth and give him some tongue when I hear a cheer. I'm sure it's Nicki, and that's what brings me back to Earth.

Our eyes meet when we break apart, and his have a little gleam to them while we both pant just a little to try to catch our breath after that epic kiss.

"Congratulations," Nicki says, handing my bouquet back to me, and Luke and I link hands while Kaylee and Tim clap for us with my parents, Nicki, and Josh—I do note, however, that Carol, Jack, and Michelle refrain from celebrating our union. They're not clapping or cheering or even smiling.

I bet those assholes will still eat the cake we paid for, though.

CHAPTER 2

It was nice of you to try to protect my heart, but Ellie already owns it.

Ellie carries my heart. She holds it in her hands, and I count myself the luckiest man in the world that I found her when I did.

If those aren't wedding vows, I'm not sure what words would be.

Did he mean them?

That's the question. If he has feelings for me...well, then I guess we could try dating. We could try getting to know one another on another level. We could give a relationship, our *marriage*, a real try.

But if he doesn't, then nothing changes.

I just can't figure out why he'd keep up the ruse when I admitted this morning that I have feelings for him. He never got the chance to tell me whether he reciprocates those feelings, but after the words he said tonight paired with the way I feel about him, I can't honestly believe he doesn't feel it, too.

It can't be one-sided.

It's too strong and too deep to be anything less than real.

We head right for our reception after we're announced as husband and wife, which is really just a small, private room at the nicest restaurant in the hotel. We're seated at a round table large enough for our entire party, and a small dance floor waits behind us. The cake is in another corner and it's all very simple. We're given menus, and I glance it over as I try to decide what the first dinner I have with my husband should be.

Luke reaches over to rest his hand on my leg once he's decided what he wants, and it's another small sign that his feelings might be real. Nobody can see his hand under the table. There's no reason for it to be there on my leg other than that he *wants* it to be there.

I almost lean in to ask if he meant what he said, but there are too many prying eyes around this table. Too many people who clearly would love nothing more than to expose the truth. And that would be extra detrimental for my husband considering Michelle is sitting across the table from us.

What a mess.

He leans over and presses a soft kiss to my cheek, the scruff on his jaw tickling me. I turn and catch his lips with mine. It's what you do when you're the bride at your wedding reception, right? I'm taking every chance I can to publicly let the people at this table know that we're in love.

And the more we kiss and touch each other and hold hands, certainly the more convincing we'll be.

Carol huffs across the table, and then she finally breaks her silence. "So you're the girl my son impregnated?"

She looks at Michelle like she's a big bug that just crawled across the table. Finally, Carol and I seem to agree on something. Michelle's eyes edge to Luke, and mine do, too. I'm pretty sure steam is coming out of his ears.

Michelle clears her throat. "Yes," she says softly, and my goodness is she milking the pregnancy card for every single ounce its worth.

"When are you due?" Carol finally asks her. It is, after all, her grandchild in there despite the horrid woman carrying it.

"December tenth," Michelle says, flashing them a sweet smile.

"Can we save this conversation for another time, please?" I ask. "We're just trying to enjoy our wedding reception, which obviously isn't about Michelle in any way despite her best effort to make it about her."

I smile sweetly at the group gathered, and I see Nicki stifle a laugh at my harsh words. But you know what? I don't give a fuck. The only people I care about at this table are my family and Luke. Everyone else can fuck off out of here, and I mean that in the sincerest way possible.

"I ended up the real winner here," I say, leaning over to kiss Luke on the cheek. "Locked this one into marriage when he said he'd never do it again. I guess he was just with the wrong woman before." I lift my wineglass haughtily to my lips, and Michelle glares at me from across the table because she knows I'm right.

She couldn't lock him down, he dumped her, so she showed back up for a bonus night and found a way to claw herself into his life forever.

God, Luke. He really picks some winners.

Thank God I entered the picture when I did. This poor man needed a decent woman in his life to stand up for him, and I will continue to do that—for the next year, at least. Maybe longer if he lets me.

I turn toward Nicki and Josh and ask about their honeymoon, effectively ending the Michelle conversation. Luke and I chat with them and my parents as they fill us in on Fiji—where, incidentally, I wish I was right now rather than at this table with most of these people. We eat, we laugh, we ignore the Daltons, and then it's time to dance. Luke holds me in his arms as we listen to "Speechless" again, dancing our first dance as husband and wife.

He kisses me, and it feels real.

Josh and Nicki join us for the bridal party song, and I don't care about the rest of them, but they join us for a few songs, too, before his parents call it a night first. Michelle's feet are *positively aching*, so she heads out. Jack and Kaylee leave with her, and I wonder if the Dalton family likes Michelle more than Luke let on.

That leaves the only people who I actually care about, but my parents bow out, then Josh and Nicki decide to call it a night, too. They're newlyweds, after all, and I don't even want to know what sort of freaky shit they're about to get up to.

And then it's finally time for the conversation I've been holding off all night.

It's time to confront my husband and find out if he has feelings for me.

CHAPTER 3

My hands tremble as we get back to our room. Will he sleep on the couch again tonight after everything that went down today?

Or will he at least give me some courtesy sex since it's our wedding night?

Yeah, I doubt that one, too.

He settles onto the couch, where he kicks off his shoes, and I settle into the chair across from him, where I take off mine, too. He's still in his suit. I'm still in my wedding gown.

"Why would Michelle come all this way to stop the wedding?" I ask. "Did she really think you'd choose her?"

He shrugs. "She was already a little unhinged. Pregnancy has made it worse, I think."

"She was unhinged?" I ask. It sounds like there's more to that story.

"She's holding onto something that hasn't been there a long time for me. I can't lie when I admit I'm concerned that she's going to make trouble for me at *the office*," he says, air quoting his last two words to indicate his relationship with her father.

A beat of quiet passes between us, and I glance up at him. "What are you thinking?"

He turns toward the window. "I don't know," he mutters. "I'm not sure if she's going to run to Daddy and fuck up my relationship even more with him."

"Why'd you start dating her in the first place?" I ask. He doesn't strike me as the kind of guy who would choose to mix business with pleasure. Example one would be how I can't seem to get him to admit there's something between us.

Eventually I'll get to that question.

He huffs out a mirthless chuckle. "We first met at a charity event. I had no idea who she was at the time. I knew Calvin had a daughter, but she'd been overseas studying fashion, so I'd never met her. She approached me and asked me out, and I liked that she had the balls to do that. It was one of the first things that attracted me to her. We went out a couple times and we slept together before I learned who her father is. I was pissed that she kept it a secret, but she had a valid point that I never would've dated her if I knew. And then I basically lost two years of my life to her. She treated me like trash, and I didn't know how to end things without pissing off her dad, so I stayed far longer than I should have while things just got more and more broken between us."

"I'm so sorry, Luke. You've had some pretty bad luck when it comes to women."

He nods as he presses his lips together. "Pretty much why I swore off marriage. Until I met you." His face smooths into a smile, and this is my chance. I take a deep breath to ask the question that's been on my mind since he said those beautiful words earlier, but he wrinkles his nose. "But I don't want to talk about Michelle anymore."

"What do you want to talk about?" I breathe. Is this it? Finally?

He shrugs and looks out the window, as if to tell me he doesn't really have a topic in mind. That's when I decide I need to get in the driver's seat.

"I need to ask you something," I finally say.

He glances over at me before he folds his hands and leans his elbows on his knees. "Go for it."

I draw in a deep breath. On the other side of this question lies my fate. If I get the answer I'm hoping for, the next year could be a dream come true—and maybe even beyond. And if I don't...well, I haven't really considered that possibility yet. But either way, I'll know.

I let out the breath slowly, and then I finally say the words I've been wondering all night. "What you said during the ceremony about how I carry your heart and you count yourself lucky...did you mean that? Or were those just more words for the show we were putting on?"

He tilts his head a little, his eyes lifting to mine from where they're pinned down toward his hands. "I meant it."

My chest tightens and my heart races as he stands.

He moves across the small space between us and holds a hand out to me. I set my hand in his, and he helps me up before he pulls me into his arms. I'm pressed against his front, and I take the lapels of the suit jacket he still wears between my hands if nothing else so I have something to grip onto.

"I meant every word," he says softly. His eyes burn down into mine, and my fingers tighten over his lapels. "I'm tired of living this lie. It's exhausting pretending like I haven't fallen in love with you, too."

He presses a soft kiss to my lips while my ears buzz and I feel a little dizzy.

He feels it too?

"I had to push you away. I had to pretend like this doesn't mean everything to me, like *you* don't mean everything to me." His voice is full of passion, a rare show of emotion that I very much trust. "And it's because of Jack. I thought if we got married in front of him, he'd believe me. But he ruins every good thing I have. He can't come in second, ever, and he will try to tear us apart. I thought if I pretended it wasn't real, like I didn't feel anything for you, it would be easier when he succeeded, because Jack *always* gets what he wants."

"Not this time," I say. I grip those lapels a little harder. "He won't tear us apart, Luke, because we were meant to find each other. We crashed into one another before we were supposed to meet because fate put you at the club that night."

"I don't believe in fate," he says. "But I do believe in feelings. I haven't been forthcoming with you, and I apologize for that. I don't know what admitting this to you will do to us over the next year, but, God, I want it to work. I want to take you to bed. I want to wake up next to you. I want it all. With you."

I brush my lips to his, finally letting go of his suit jacket to link my arms around him. His body is flush against mine, right where it should be...where it hasn't been for far too long.

"So why is this suddenly okay?" I ask against his lips, not sure why I'm questioning it but needing the whole truth before I get my hopes up too high.

"Because I'm so fucking tired of pretending. I love you, Ellie. I'm so damn in love with you. We're doing this all backwards, and I know you're my wife now, but I'd love to take you out on a date. I want to get to know you as more than just my best friend's sister, as more than just my roommate, as more than just my publicist." He peppers soft kisses between phrases.

"Hawaii seems like a nice place to get our fresh start," I say, and then there's no more talking.

He kisses me like he did when Manny announced us as husband and wife down on the beach, but this time no one stops us when our mouths open and our tongues brush together.

His grip around my waist tightens, and then out of nowhere, he sweeps me up into his arms and carries me into the bedroom. "Tonight won't be about palms on windows or taking you from behind. Tonight's a night to celebrate this new union between us." He presses a soft kiss to my lips as my heart races and a wave of emotion plows through me.

He sets me on my feet rather than on the bed, and then he spins me around so he's looking at the back of my dress.

He doesn't touch it yet—just merely seems to be staring at it. "Is there a lock on this thing?"

I giggle. The layers of lace on top bury the tiny buttons that close the back, and it took Nicki a good five minutes to get them all buttoned up. I didn't stop to think how I'd get *out* of it, and especially not with such intense need between my new husband and me.

I'd suggest just going up the bottom and getting busy right here in my dress, but the layers of chiffon and silk will make that a difficult feat.

"The buttons are under the lace," I say, and he fingers the back until he uncovers them.

"Jesus Christ," he mutters when he sees the sheer number.

"I'm sorry," I say.

He chuckles as he gets to work. "Don't be. You look gorgeous. The most beautiful bride I've ever seen in my life." I feel the back starting to open as he pushes each button patiently, slowly through each loop. He's calm and collected while the thought of what's coming sends nerves through my entire system.

We've done this before, but that first time, it was meaningless. This time...it's not.

"When I first saw you walking down the aisle toward me, I had a feeling this was how our night was going to end. Whether you asked me about my real feelings or not...I was going to confess them."

Another button through the loop, another thump in my chest.

"It wasn't just your beauty," he says, "but the way you carried yourself with such beautiful, calm, simple grace." He presses a kiss to the small gap he's made as he keeps progressing down the buttons. "It was the way you stood up beside me and I felt like we could face anything together. And we did. We faced my family. We faced Michelle." He slips another button through. "Done," he says with another soft kiss to my back, and he spins me back around.

I slip his jacket off his arms, and it falls into a pile on the floor. I unbutton his shirt, my fingers shaking as I make slow progress. He's patient as I work, and he sets to unbuttoning the cuffs of his shirt. He sets the cufflinks on the dresser behind him as I get to the last button, and then I slide his shirt down his arms and it falls on top of the jacket.

I take a minute to stare at his abs.

Holy shit. I'm married to those.

For the next year, at least.

And now that he's confessed how he really feels, I'm going to enjoy every damn minute of this union.

CHAPTER 4

He slides the straps of my dress slowly down my arms, and it drifts from my arms to the ground. My heart pounds so hard I'm certain he can see it beneath the white lace lingerie set I wore under the gown *just in case*.

I've wanted this to happen again since the first time, and now that it's actually happening, I'm a nervous wreck. It's a mixture of *will it be as good as the first time* and *oh my God we're really doing this* and *holy hell we're* married *now*.

The fear that I somehow won't be good enough for him is real and tangible.

He stares at me for a beat, and the self-conscious side feels like he's studying me. "So perfect," he murmurs, and then moves in toward me and presses a kiss to my neck. "I love you, Mrs. Dalton," he says.

"I love you, too," I say on a moan as his lips move from my neck down into my cleavage. He's moving slowly, deliberately, with love and tenderness—something missing from the first time we did this. It was savage and hot and fiery. There was no fear of what tomorrow might bring because it didn't matter when it was just supposed to be for one night.

But something brought us together. He might not believe in fate...but I do.

We were meant to find one another ahead of time. We were meant to have this history between us as we traveled on our journey, and maybe we're at the destination now. Maybe this is where our happily ever after begins.

It might be naïve to think that way, but it's what I'm choosing to believe tonight.

He sweeps me up into his arms and carries me to the bed, his lips finding mine as he moves the short distance, and if that's not a damn fairy tale Prince Charming move for the books, I'm not sure what is. He lays me down gently and moves so he's hovering over me. His eyes burn into mine for a beat, and then his fingertips run down my torso, landing on my thigh. He settles between my legs, still wearing pants, and he thrusts his hips toward me as he buries his face in my cleavage.

A little moan escapes me. As good as this feels, I want him. All of him. I want our clothes out of the way, and I want him pounding into me as I lie beneath him. I didn't get to feel his warmth over me the first time. I didn't get to look into his eyes, to watch his handsome face screw up with pleasure instead of his reflection in the window.

I'm not missing those things this time.

His lips land back on mine, our tongues battering together as he continues thrusting his hips to mine, both of us moaning as the frenzy between us builds to nearly unbearable levels, an ache pressing between my thighs as needy moans escape me.

He stops abruptly and stands, unbuckling his belt and lowering his pants and boxers. He stands naked before me for only the second time, but it's incredible how different the feelings are this time. I won't need to scrub away the guilt in the morning.

Does it still qualify as a one-night stand when you *marry* the guy?

"Slight problem," he says. "I didn't bring any condoms. I figured less temptation that way."

CHAPTER 5

That old phrase *cloud nine* has nothing on where I'm floating when I wake up in the morning. Not only am I married, but I'm married to the guy I've fallen in love with...and he's in love with me, too.

When I was fired and Todd dumped me twelve seconds later, I thought it would be a long-ass time before I found happiness again, yet here I am, less than two months later. Happy as a damn clam.

Until Luke wakes up and opens his mouth. "We probably shouldn't have done that," he says instead of something simple like *good morning* or *hey there wife* or even *should we do that again?*

I blow out a breath and get out of bed angrily. "Are you serious, Luke?" I grab a shirt and pull it on because you're damn right if you think we slept naked.

"It's just going to complicate our agreement," he says, like that's any better.

I shake my head sadly as the anger starts to dissipate into pure disappointment. "I should believe you when you keep telling me you're no prince. Maybe you're right. But you sure fuck like one." I mutter the last part and I leave those as my parting words as I head to the bathroom, slam the door, and take a shower.

It's sort of like the last time we were together. I scrubbed and scrubbed under scalding hot water, but nothing could make the grime go away. The same holds true this time.

No matter how hard I scrub, I can't change what he just said.

I can't try to justify his hurtful words.

He knocks on the bathroom door just as I finish drying off. I wrap the fluffy hotel bathrobe around me and open the door. "What?" I spit at him.

He gives me a wry smile, and why does he have to be so goddamn hot? I can't stay mad at him when he looks at me like that. It's like a damn puppy dog with sad eyes.

"I'm sorry. I guess I've just gotten used to pushing people away, but I don't want to push you away. I just don't know how to be in a real relationship."

I weigh my options here. I could give in and set the precedent that it's okay to say mean things to me, or I could stand my ground.

I go with the latter. I have to.

"You're right," I say. "You don't know how. And it might just be part of my job description to teach you."

"How can I make it up to you?" he asks.

"Find another hotel," I say, standing my ground. "Our honeymoon starts today, and it starts away from your toxic family. I want more nights like we had last night and less mornings like we're having right now."

"Consider it done. What else?"

"You once told me that there were two people in your failed relationships. What did you do that caused them to end?" I ask.

"Oh Jesus," he says. "It's too damn early for this conversation."

I raise a brow.

He blows out a breath. "Fine. But can we at least order breakfast first?"

I nod toward the phone and cross my arms over my chest. "You know what I like."

He gives me a look I can't quite decode, and then he walks over and picks up the phone. I grab my clothes and close the bathroom door while he orders.

Time to find out if he's been paying attention.

After I finish getting ready, I pack up my toiletries with a sigh. I don't *really* want to leave this place. It is, after all, where we got married yesterday. But my family is heading out today, and with his family and Michelle here, I can't stay. Not when they constantly hurt him, and not if we're meant to enjoy this "honeymoon." It's a big place, but not big enough to escape all that.

I toss my make-up bag in my suitcase and start reorganizing my clothes when Luke appears in the bedroom doorway holding a cup of coffee. He isn't wearing a shirt, his hair is messy from sleep, and the light is hitting him at the most perfect angle. He looks like a damn advertisement for coffee.

I slip my phone out of my pocket and snap a picture.

"What was that for?" he asks.

"I swear, if you didn't play football, you could model," I murmur, checking out the picture I just took—another one for the spank bank, not that I need it if he's going to deliver like last night again. I push that whole *we shouldn't have done that* thing out of my head and try not to read past what he said.

"I'm ready to talk now," he says, lifting his coffee cup into the air to indicate that he couldn't really get moving on conversation until he had that in hand.

I nod, and I follow him out toward the couch where he *didn't* sleep last night. I set to work on my own cup of coffee, too. He collapses onto the couch, and I sit in the chair across from him.

"So what I said this morning, about our agreement...it's shit like that, Ellie. I work hard to push people away. Sometimes I blame my family for that, and sometimes I think it's just all me."

"Why do you think you do that?"

He lifts a shoulder and looks out the window. "When it comes to women, it's usually because of Jack. But fuck the agreement. I want to give this a real try with you."

"Then I need to understand your past. Start with Savannah." I take a small sip of my piping hot coffee, proud of myself for being blunt about what I need out of this relationship.

"Like I said, it usually goes back to Jack. He was just always there between Savannah and me, and I always wondered if I was good enough since she was with him first," he admits. He sits up a little straighter, palming his coffee cup in both hands.

"Why'd you marry her?" I ask, truly wondering what the answer might be.

He clears his throat, and his eyes move to mine. He regards me for a beat, studies me like he's trying to decide if he can trust me. "I thought I loved her."

"*Thought?*" I ask.

He nods. "We were, uh, sleeping together when I tore my ACL in the middle of my second season."

"I didn't know you tore your ACL," I say, not sure why that matters.

"I was out the rest of the season. I missed most of training camp and preseason my third year, but I was ready for the field by our home opener." He presses his lips together.

"How'd you feel about being out?" I ask.

His eyes turn back to the window. "It was the hardest eight months of my life. Savannah took care of me, and I guess along the way, I developed real feelings for her. Eventually, I proposed."

"So how did you start sleeping with her when you knew she'd been with your brother?"

A knock at the door saves him from answering. "Room service," the voice on the other side says.

Luke gets up to let in the attendant, who wheels in a cart with our food. He signs the receipt and the attendant leaves while I pull the lids off the plates.

I wrinkle my nose at the egg white omelet with a bunch of vegetables including spinach, and I smile at the plate of pancakes, scrambled eggs, and hash browns.

I knew he'd pick right.

"The omelet is for you," he says, coming up behind me and setting his hands on my hips.

I giggle, and he nips a soft kiss on my neck, and somehow any lasting anger I had from his words this morning seems to melt away.

We sit to eat, and I bring up my question from a few minutes ago. "Back to Savannah. How did you first get together?"

"She and Jack had broken up a few weeks earlier." He takes a bite of omelet. "They lived in San Diego, and I went to stay with Jack a few days before our family trip to Vancouver. This was back when we were close. I had literally *just* had a conversation with my brother about how he didn't want the same things she did. She wanted marriage and kids and the white picket fence, and he wanted to play the field and have some fun. He was out, and she stopped by to talk to him and got me instead. She was crying, all upset, yada yada yada. We exchanged numbers, and it started out very innocently but quickly turned into talking every day. Eventually I was in San Diego again and we went to dinner. She took me back to her place, and the rest is history."

"How did Jack react when he found out?" I ask.

"He said he didn't care."

I raise a brow. "But he did?"

Luke shrugs.

I let that slide because the truth is that these brothers will *never* have an even score between them. "Okay, so you dated, got hurt, got engaged, got married. And then things fell apart?" I ask.

"Sort of." He cuts some of his omelet with his fork but sets down his fork instead of eating it. "She didn't just want marriage. She wanted to be a football wife. She wanted money. She chased fame. And I helped her chase that fame when I let her write that series on Jack and me."

I dip my pancake into the syrup. "And you had no inclination about any of that before you married her?"

He shakes his head. "I'm sure this isn't something you want to hear, but I was blinded by the sex."

I raise a brow as I keep my eyes down on my pancakes. I'm not sure what to say to that, so a beat of quiet passes between us while I chew. And then I finally ask, "So what led to the divorce?"

"I've already talked a little about her role in that, but for my own part..." He blows out a breath. "She knew things about my family, so I had to find a way to keep her quiet. At the same time, I started to hate her. I didn't want to be married to her anymore. I couldn't. I didn't fight for us because there was nothing left to fight for. She turned into someone I didn't know, but I did, too. I pushed her away, did little things to piss her off to get her to leave first. She wouldn't budge. Eventually I offered to pay her just to get rid of her. I'm not proud of that, but I *am* proud of the fact that I didn't have as much then as I do now. I threw myself into work, and the year after our divorce was my best season up to that point."

"Don't you sort of *have to* throw yourself into work, though?" I ask, tucking the need to know more regarding these secrets about his family into the back of my mind for now.

"Well, yes and no," he says. He lifts his coffee cup to his lips for a quick sip. "I worked out constantly. More than I needed to. I was in the best shape of my life. Looking back, I did it as a means to escape her and to escape the way she made me feel. I was angry all the time. She put this divide between Jack and me that hadn't existed before. She caused a split in my family. I admit a large part of the blame falls on my shoulders there, too. Then the team offered me my current contract worth more than she and I ever dreamed of. The best part? She didn't get to touch that money. But it led to an even bigger issue with her."

"Why?" I ask, and I think I know the answer, but I wait with bated breath for his answer.

"Because of what she knows."

"What does she know?" I breathe.

He shakes his head and keeps his gaze down. "Enough about Savannah," he murmurs. He's not spilling those family secrets today, but my curiosity burns.

"So we're moving onto Michelle?" I flash him a smile.

"Good try." He finishes the last bite of his omelet. "But we have to save *something* for lunch conversation, don't you think?"

"I figured we'd talk about all *my* failed relationships at lunch."

He wrinkles his nose. "What if I don't want to know?"

"You already know about Todd. The rest were all pretty short-term. Nothing nearly as exciting as yours."

He laughs. "Fair enough. But to be honest, when it comes to why things failed with Michelle, it's basically the same story without the marriage. We tried, we both turned into different people, and it just didn't work out. Rather than allowing family secrets to be the thing holding me back from breaking up with her, it was the fact that she's my boss's daughter. I held on as long as I could, but I think I'm just not one of those people who's destined to have relationships that last longer than a year."

Enter Ellie.

"Hence the one-year contract?" I ask.

He shrugs. "I figured if nothing else, you could put up with me for a year, and vice versa. But that was when we were friends. Throwing sex and feelings into the mix will definitely complicate things, and that's all I meant this morning when I said that. I didn't mean to hurt your feelings, but like I've told you, I don't know how to do relationships. People leave. People choose Jack, and not just women. I've had buddies who chose him. My own damn family chose him." He shrugs. "Why would you be any different?"

"Because I love *you*, Luke," I say, my voice full of all the passion I've had to push away for the last few weeks since I first realized I was falling for him. "I don't give a shit about football. You're my brother's best friend, and you've helped me out, and I fell for the person *you* are long before I met him. I don't care about your job or your money or your brother or your family or any of that stuff. I just care about you."

He stares at me a long beat like he's trying to gauge whether my words are the truth. "I care about you, too."

"Lesson one for an adult relationship. You ready? You listening good?" I ask.

He chuckles and nods.

"Okay. Don't push me away. Don't bow out. Talk to me, and fight with me, and communicate with me. It's the only way relationships work." Not that I'm any expert, to be honest. Just look at Todd.

But Luke and I have the tools to make this work, and now that he's let me into a small part of his history, I'm ready to get on with the honeymoon.

CHAPTER 6

We're standing at the reception desk in the lobby a little before lunch time when we hear Kaylee's voice from across the lobby.

"What are you doing?" she asks. She's in her swimwear, sunglasses perched on her head. I'd feel sorry for her that she's stuck with Carol, Tim, Jack, and Michelle for the next few days, but she betrayed us when she ran to Jack with what she heard, so I can't muster up those feelings of sympathy.

"Checking out," Luke says thickly. He signs the receipt and pushes it back toward the clerk, who hands him back a folder with our suite charges.

"Thank you for staying with us," the clerk says, and Luke nods before we both turn to face Kaylee.

"Where are you going?" she asks.

"On our honeymoon," Luke says, tossing an arm around my shoulders to draw me in closer, "and we can't do that here in a place filled with traitors and people who want our relationship to fail."

"But...but..." she sputters. "Luke, this is our family trip. You can't just leave."

"Watch me."

Carol and Tim, also donning swim gear, saunter up behind Kaylee, and this is the exact reason we're leaving. This place is too damn small to enjoy the time we have left on this island.

Carol's brow is raised. "Where are you two off to?"

"They're checking out," Kaylee says, ever the little tattletale.

"We're going to another hotel to enjoy what's left of our trip. Just the two of us." He leans over and presses a kiss to my temple.

Carol rolls her eyes. "Still keeping up the act, I see."

"It's not an act," Luke says. Our eyes meet, and in this moment, I know he's telling the truth. That's how it started, and we're certainly not in the position for a traditional marriage given how long we've known one another...but at this point, we're both committed to giving it a real try. And that's what makes it so much more than the *act* we each signed up for.

"Okay," she says, her tone full of sarcasm. "So why leave this lovely place?"

"Do you really want the answer to that?" Luke asks. "Enjoy your day at the beach. Enjoy the rest of your trip. Enjoy your life. I don't know if I can be a part of any of it anymore."

A spear of sadness forms in me. As much as my mom drives me crazy, I still love her. I'd never just part ways with her. But watching the way Luke's family treats him makes me see how families can become estranged. I try to think of it from their perspective, and I still can't wrap my head around why they constantly degrade him while building up his brother. It's not right, and maybe now that he has me, he can finally start to see that he deserves more.

Luke sighs as he turns away from his family, and together we walk away from them and toward the restaurant where we're meeting my family for lunch before they check out to head home and we head to our new hotel to check in.

They don't try to stop us. They don't say anything else—not even in response to Luke's words that he can't be a part of their lives anymore.

That spear of sadness I felt before seems stronger. If I feel it, I can't imagine what he's feeling.

At least we didn't run into Jack.

Yet.

"Are you okay?" I ask once we're out of earshot.

He nods and presses his lips together. "Better than I've been in a long time, I think." He leans over and kisses me. It's soft and quick, just a nip of lip to lip, but it feels like so much more. It's sealing our promise. It's a thank you for holding his hand through that. And maybe, above all, it's not for show. He kissed me because he wanted to, not because we're faking for everyone. That one was just for us, just as all the kisses in our future will be.

I just wish we didn't have the heavy cloud of what just happened with his family hanging over us.

Nicki and Josh are already seated and waiting for us when we slide into the chairs across from them. "There's the newlyweds," Nicki says, and I smile. "Did you two have a crazy kinky night?"

Josh wrinkles his nose. "Babe, gross. That's my sister."

"And it's my best friend," Nicki points out. "I need all the details."

"You know it's not real, right?" Josh whispers to her, loud enough for only Luke and me to hear as I wave over my parents when I spot them near the hostess stand at the front of the restaurant.

"Actually..." Luke says, and then he turns to me. His eyes twinkle despite what just happened, and I get the sense that a weight lifted when he said those words to his parents. He seems a little lighter despite the heaviness I still feel.

"Oh my God," Nicki squeals.

"What?" Josh asks.

Luke kisses me again and then turns to my brother. "I'm in love with your sister."

Josh's eyes practically bug out of his head. "You...this is...wait. You are? For real?" He glances at Nicki. "See? I told you!"

Luke laughs. "I am. And I'm sorry. I know I promised you I wouldn't take a shot at her."

Josh looks between the two of us, and he seems to soften a little. "This seems like more than *taking a shot.*"

"It is," Luke says softly as he grabs my hand in his.

My parents approach the table and we all stand for good morning hugs.

I still can't quite get over the contrast from his family to mine.

Once we're all seated again, Luke regards my parents. He seems suddenly nervous as he clears his throat. He glances around and sees that we're alone in our little corner of the restaurant before he speaks. "Mr. and Mrs. Nolan, I just wanted to thank you both for being here, and I also wanted to let you know that last night I told your daughter about my real feelings for her. I'm in love with her, and we're both thrilled to be giving this a real shot."

My parents glance at each other, and then they both look at me. "Is this what you want?" my dad asks.

I can't help my grin as I nod. "More than anything." My eyes edge over to my husband. "I'm so in love with Luke."

My mom squeals and claps her hands together. "Does that mean I'm finally getting a grandchild sometime soon?"

I laugh as Luke blanches. "One step at a time, Mom," I say. I jab my thumb toward my brother and Nicki. "Maybe badger these two a while first."

Josh blanches a bit, too, and then Nicki throws the attention back to me by changing the subject as she clears her throat. "So what's next for you two?"

"We just checked out of here and we're going to another hotel to celebrate our honeymoon," I say.

"Away from my toxic family," Luke adds.

"You both deserve to be happy," Josh says. "I'm glad you're finding that with each other. But keep the details to yourself, okay?"

We all get a good laugh out of that. We order, and so far, we haven't had the pleasure of running into the last member of Luke's family that we haven't said goodbye to just yet. My fingers are crossed that we don't...but that would be too easy, wouldn't it?

My parents are at the reception desk checking out. It's as we're hugging Josh and Nicki in the lobby and bidding them a safe trip home—a place that doesn't sound so bad right now—before they head up to pack to catch the flight they're all taking together that we hear Jack's voice.

"The party's over so soon?"

I draw in a deep breath before I turn around. Michelle is right by his side, and the prissy gloating expression on her face makes me want to barf.

"We're heading home tonight," Josh says, and he seems to regard Jack a little warily. I'm not sure if that caution has more to do with the fact that he's professional competition or with how Jack treats Luke. Maybe both.

"And we're heading to another hotel," Luke says.

Jack's brows arch. "Running away?"

Luke grunts out a chuckle. "Hardly. I'd just like to enjoy my honeymoon with my new bride away from my family and Michelle."

"So...running away," Jack says.

"Sure," Luke says, and his tone clearly expresses that he doesn't care what his brother thinks.

And *that* might just be the deepest dig for Jack. He doesn't know how to respond to his brother's sarcastic indifference, and seeing him sputter for a beat is somehow totally out of character for him while it's incredibly satisfying to watch.

Luke glances between Michelle and Jack. He narrows his eyes at them. "Hope you're enjoying your sloppy seconds."

Jack raises a brow and lowers his voice. "I'll let you know once I get Ellie into my bed." He winks at me.

"That will *never* happen," I snarl.

Josh steps in to save the day as my parents join us. "Well, you two have a fun honeymoon. We'll see you when you're back home."

I give each member of my family one final hug, and then I wiggle my fingers at Jack and Michelle while Luke gives them a smirk.

"Bye," we say together, and then we head out for the car waiting for us out front to take us to our new hotel.

CHAPTER 7

"What's a *lanai*?" I ask.

Luke types the word into his browser on his phone before reading me the results. "The Hawaiian word for *porch* or *veranda*."

"Well whatever it is, I'm in love with it." I collapse into one of the cushioned chairs on our *lanai* that overlooks the ocean. If I thought the last hotel was nice, well, it has nothing on this one.

This one boasts *nine* pools with waterslides, a lazy river, and waterfalls, seven restaurants, and beach access all in the lap of luxury. Our huge suite has a private lanai, and it's both relaxing and romantic...and, maybe most importantly, it's just for us. We may still be on the same island as the rest of his family, but this separation feels both necessary and much better.

It's ours, and ours alone, for the next week.

We spend our days at the pool and our nights naked. We relax. We fall asleep on the beach. We cover each other in sunscreen. We swim. We ride waterslides and kiss under waterfalls. We learn how to kayak. We snorkel. We get massages. We have sex up against windows and in our bed and in the shower and he even slips it in when we're in the ocean, separated by ourselves yet with people all around us probably doing the same thing.

We spend time together laughing, the weight of his family and their secrets mixed with what started as a lie between us off our shoulders as we truly get to explore everything about each other for the first time.

I don't know if I've ever felt closer to another person. There are still secrets he holds, but they have no bearing on us. Maybe someday he'll be ready to tell me about them, and maybe not. I'm not sure if it matters. They're swept away with history, and I keep telling myself that they don't *really* matter...even though a small part of me hates that Savannah still holds onto a piece of him that he doesn't want to reveal to me.

It's still early days for us. We have at least a year or the rest of our lives.

The seven remaining days of our honeymoon in Hawaii pass in the blink of an eye without drama and without incident, and suddenly I find myself staring out Luke's car window as he pulls back onto his street. We're nearly *home*. When we left, I'd just signed a contract saying this would be home for the next year, and now I have hope that it might last far beyond that.

I'm excited to get back to work. I'm ready to sort through our photos, to focus on our upcoming charity event, to make my new husband indispensable to his team...even to make his team owner see that marrying me was the right choice despite Luke having knocked up his daughter. That might be a stretch, but if anyone can do it convincingly, it's me.

He pulls into the driveaway, and I can't wait to get inside, kiss Pepper on the head, and unpack the luggage. I'm tired of living out of suitcases...but even if I wasn't, it's just in my nature to have everything unpacked, the laundry started, and the suitcases put away within an hour after arriving home.

"Look who's back," a singsong voice from next door calls as we pull suitcases out of the back of the car.

"Hey, Mrs. Adams," Luke says. He doesn't stop what he's doing to acknowledge her, further evidence that he's ready to just be home, too.

"You know you're supposed to call me Dorothy," she reminds him. She looks between the two of us. "I saw the gossip columns, but please tell me they got it wrong. You didn't go and get *married* now, did you?"

Luke holds up the shiny new hardware on the third finger of his left hand. "We sure did." He flashes her a cheesy smile and draws me in with an arm around my shoulders.

"Tsk tsk," she tuts. "Abigail will be so disappointed."

"Tell your granddaughter I'm so sorry, but I fell in love," Luke says, his eyes on me.

"Can I still sit on your lap at least?" she taunts, and Luke laughs.

"No. But if you need a pickle jar opened, you know I'm your guy."

"I hope you two are happy," she says. "As happy as you and Savannah were, at the very least."

"Now, Mrs. Adams, you know that's not a nice thing to say," he admonishes.

She holds up her hands, the picture of innocence. I know she's basically harmless, but that doesn't mean I have to like the way she hits on my husband.

"Mrs. Adams?" I say. She turns her attention to me, and she looks at me like I'm a naughty toddler. "My brother across the street is real good with pickle jars, too." I smile sweetly, and then I turn into my husband and plant a big kiss on his mouth.

Here's to hoping that shuts her up.

Luke lugs the heavier bags upstairs and I take up our carry-ons once he opens the door. I immediately set to unpacking.

"What are you doing?" he asks.

"Unpacking," I say. "Why? What does it look like?"

"Don't you want to relax a little?" he asks. "Debbie's bringing food plus Pepper by in an hour. We can do this later."

I purse my lips and shake my head. "There are two types of people in this world, Luke. We have those who unpack immediately when they get home, and we have those who leave their bags untouched for days. Which are you?"

"The first one?" he guesses, and I nod.

"Good boy. Now get unpacked. There's no relaxing until this is done."

"Yes, ma'am," he says.

"See? Prince Charming."

He laughs as he starts separating his clean clothes from the dirties.

"Doing my best," he says.

I stand and walk over to him. I loop my arms around his neck. "You're doing great. Thank you for a wonderful honeymoon. It was the best one I've ever had."

He laughs. "I know you're just saying that because it's your only one, but it was the best one I ever had, too."

I smile. "That line is *almost* good enough to get you laid, but only after you finish unpacking."

CHAPTER 8

When Debbie lets Pepper off her leash in the foyer, she bounds through the house and heads right for her daddy.

"Pepper girl!" Luke exclaims as she crashes into him. He laughs as she licks his face.

"Hey Pepper!" I say with tons of enthusiasm, ready for some puppy kisses of my own...but she's too busy with her dad.

I roll my eyes, and Debbie laughs. "Just wait until you two have children. Same thing. Dads get *all* the glory."

"You have kids?" I ask.

She nods. "My daughter is twenty-six and my son is twenty-three. They're both still here in Vegas, so I see them often."

"How nice." I scratch Pepper behind the ears. She only comes to me for a courtesy pet, and I don't get the same kisses Luke got. I'll take it.

"Thanks for taking care of her," Luke says.

"Happy to do it." She smiles. "My house is awfully quiet these days."

"You need a dog," Luke teases.

Debbie laughs. "I'll just borrow Pepper every now and again."

We all watch as Pepper jumps on the couch, walks in a circle, and settles in for her afternoon nap.

"I've got food and groceries in the car for you two. Let me just go grab everything," Debbie says.

"I'll get it." Luke moves toward the door before she gets a chance to protest.

"Congratulations on the wedding." Debbie winks at me as soon as Luke is out of earshot. "I know you'll take good care of my Luke."

"I promise." I hold a hand over my heart.

"You're good for him. I haven't seen him smile like he does around you in a very long time. Maybe ever."

"How long have you been cooking for him?" I ask.

She moves into the kitchen, and I follow her. "Oh, six or seven years now I think. He and Savannah were married when I started."

"How'd you two meet?"

"My husband was an assistant coach for years and years," she says. "He'd have meetings with the wide receivers at our house once a week and I'd cook them dinner when they were over. Luke was always such a special boy. So grateful, so kind." He comes back in at that moment with the food from Debbie's car.

"You must be talking about someone else," he jokes, and Debbie laughs as he sets the bags on the counter.

"When my husband passed, I quit cooking for the team. And then Luke offered me a job cooking for him," she says.

"She's like a mother to me." He squeezes her shoulders like he's giving her a massage. "Always telling me what to do."

She bats his hands away affectionately, and I see more mother and son love between these two in this cute little moment than I did between Carol and him the entire time we were in Hawaii.

So Debbie is a mother figure. His teammates are like brothers to him. His coaches are probably father figures at least to some degree. Maybe he was born into the Dalton family, something he couldn't choose...but it seems like he's created his own little family when he was more or less exiled from his own blood relatives.

And now he has me. The princess with her trusty animal sidekick here to save the day—or something along those lines. I guess Pepper is more of a sidekick to *him* than me, but since I know the rules of fairy tales so well, it's probably okay if I break a few.

"Are you hungry?" he asks me once Debbie leaves.

I glance at the clock. I'm still on Hawaii time, which means that even though the clock here says it's seven o'clock, it feels like four. "Sure. What did Debbie make us?"

He opens the fridge, which Debbie stocked while we finished unpacking and started the laundry. "We've got chicken, burgers, spaghetti, chili, fish..."

"Spaghetti," I say, and he takes out the container and sets to work on plating it. I grab some garlic bread from the freezer and get the oven preheating.

"What was your favorite part of the trip?" he asks.

"Definitely the wedding," I say, and I pull apart the bread and set it on a cookie sheet.

"The first or the second?"

I glance up and meet his eyes. "The real one. The one that was just for us, and then the words you said at the second one, and then, obviously, the wedding night. What was yours?"

"All the sex," he murmurs. "I want more."

I laugh. "Way to beat around the bush."

"The only bush I'll be beating on is yours."

"Whoa, Tiger," I say. "At least let me eat first."

He laughs, but when his eyes meet mine, the twinkle turns heated. "Refuel. And then you're mine."

He's not lying about that. We eat, and I brush my teeth because who wants to fuck garlic breath, and then we meet in bed.

Our bed.

The bed we've shared so many nights already while pretending like there wasn't this huge, beautiful thing between us—but we don't have to pretend anymore. It's still there between us, but we've both acknowledged it now.

And there's nothing more beautiful than when my husband strips me out of my clothes, licks his way through my pussy as he sends me to heights I've never visited before, then fucks me into oblivion.

After a hot and steamy session, he runs a bath for me. We luxuriate together in the bubbles, drinking wine as we take turns soaping each other. He holds me in his arms after he slips into bed beside me, and I'm still in his arms in the morning after a long and restful sleep for both of us.

And then it's back to reality.

I spend Monday morning working on the charity event while Luke heads to the practice facility to meet with his coach and teammates. I have under three weeks to launch this event, and four weeks from today, training camp begins for him. I have no idea what life will be like once he's at camp all day, and then a month later, the season starts.

He gets home a little after four, and I'm still in the office chipping away at this charity event. I've sent invitations to everyone on Luke's guest list, which is mostly comprised of his teammates, and I'm staring at the short list of names I came up with.

Calvin Bennett.
Michelle Bennett.
Savannah Buck.
Jack Dalton.
Tim and Carol Dalton.
Kaylee Dalton.

All people Luke did *not* include on his list. All people neither of us really want here.

But also...all people who this charity could benefit from. All people we'd be showing goodwill toward as we also show how happy we are...not that his family deserves any goodwill, especially considering how much of a weight was lifted after we left the hotel we shared with them.

I'm torn, so when he gets home, I decide to ask his opinion.

"Honey, I'm home," he sings, peeking his head into my office.

"Welcome home. Now have a seat," I say, nodding to the chair sitting across from my desk.

He raises a brow but does as instructed. "Am I in trouble?"

I chuckle. "No. I just wanted to give you an update on our event. Invitations were sent out to everyone on your list, but I thought of a few others who you didn't include."

He raises a brow. "Such as?"

"Calvin."

He shakes his head and starts to protest, but I jump in.

"You need harmony with him, Luke. Inviting the entire team and coaching staff and leaving him out looks petty, and besides, it'll give him a chance to see you're serious about doing your part for the baby even though you're married. Happily, I might add."

"The only way it'll show that I'm doing my part for the baby is if we also invite Michelle," he points out.

"Oh, good idea," I say, scribbling her name down like I hadn't thought of it.

"Ellie, no," he says.

"Come on, Luke," I say, sure this is a terrible idea but pressing it anyway. "We need to extend the olive branch. We need to be the bigger people here. And besides, Calvin probably has the fattest bank account of anyone on this list." I don't need to reiterate how *that* fact could benefit our little charity.

He huffs out a breath. "Next you're going to tell me you want to invite my family, too."

I raise a brow. "Now that you mention it..."

"No, Ellie. A firm, hard no."

"At least Jack? Think how great that'll look going into boot camp. You and your brother at a public event? The press will eat it up."

"The press? You mean Savannah, don't you." His voice is flat.

"Yep. Let's get all your enemies in one place and watch the fireworks." I flash him a smile. "Come on, it'll be fun."

"It will *not* be fun."

"You'll be too busy to care what they're doing. You can hang with your buddies, and I'll take care of the rest. Come on, Luke. I'm trying to find a way to make peace between you and your boss. To keep you here in Vegas playing for the Aces. A charity event where you're helping the community while also smoothing things over with those who have wronged you makes you not just the bigger man, but it's what will catapult your status as indispensable fan favorite."

He sighs. "You've already made up your mind, haven't you?"

I nod. "Yep."

"You've already sent them invitations, haven't you?" he asks.

I laugh. "No. I was waiting for your input first."

He narrows his eyes at me. "Were you?"

I shrug. "Not really. I'm going to do it either way, but I'd like to do it with your permission."

He sighs. "I'm never, ever going to say it's a good idea for the two of us, my brother, the girl I knocked up along with her father-slash-my boss, and my ex-wife all to attend the same event, let alone an event with my name on it. Don't you see how fucked up that is?"

"Definitely." I tap my pen on a pad of paper. "And it's also a publicist's dream, Luke. The way we handle this will pave the way for how we handle every single future event. It's telling the world, including your boss, whose shit list you are already on, that raising money for charity is more important than petty differences."

"I don't think knocking up his daughter and refusing to marry her is a *petty* difference," he points out.

"So why'd you really marry me?" I ask, trying to get to the root of this.

He glances away from me, like it'll soften the blow of the truth even though I'm fully aware of what I signed on for. "You offered me the only way out of being trapped by Michelle into something I didn't want. I take full responsibility for the child we'll share. I will love that kid with everything I have. But that doesn't mean I have to be with Michelle. Trust me when I say that the two of us together would be toxic for a child. Whatever happens between you and me, at least we both have an out at the end of it. With her...she wasn't about to let me have that, and neither would her father if he had anything to say about it."

"Then how great would it look for you to invite them both to this thing? To show them they have a place in your life, the baby has a place here, and you can still be one big happy family without having to commit to Michelle?" I set my pen down and fold my hands on top of my desk. "It's the best of all worlds. It smooths things over with her dad, it shows you're making a real effort. But leaving them off the guest list does the exact opposite."

He thinks about that a few beats, and then he finally sighs and nods. "You're right."

I wink at him. "Get used to saying that."

He rolls his eyes, and I shrug innocently.

"Happy wife, happy life...right?" I ask.

"Something like that," he mutters. "But when this whole thing blows up, it's on you."

"I am willing to shoulder that so long as when it *doesn't* blow up and you raise a ton of dough for your new foundation, that's also on me."

"Deal," he says, and he sticks his hand out across my desk. I shake it. "I have more questions. Have you considered holding this event indoors somewhere or is it definitely an outdoor event?"

"Of course," I say. "I found one affordable indoor option since, as you know, it's hot as fuck in the summer in Vegas, but I reserved a local park. Indoors means fancier, and that's not what you said you wanted. This way, people can bring their families, and we can hold it somewhere that's similar to what you want to build for other parts of our community. I'm thinking we can set up tents for the players with extra air coolers, other tents for drinking and hanging out, and maybe a bounce house for the kids. It'll be a charity event unlike any our guests have ever been to. It'll be the event of the season, and maybe next year, we'll find a date when we can hold it in sub-triple digit temps."

"Are you sure you want to rush this?" he asks, folding his arms across his chest.

I nod. "I think we have to. We need this to take place before the season while you have time to do it. We have to prove now what an asset you are to this community. And I promise, I'll do it right."

"I know you will." He exhales. "And on a totally different note, your brother and Nicki are coming over for a date night in an hour."

"Tonight?" I ask. To be honest, I've been working all damn day. I'm tired, and I want a glass of wine and maybe a foot massage from my new husband in the bathtub...but instead, I'm supposed to be entertaining?

"Yeah. Is that a problem?"

"Nope. Can't wait." I smile sweetly. If he can budge a little on the whole inviting all the worst people in the world to his summer outdoor charity event, I suppose I can give up my foot massage in the tub idea. Seems like a pretty even trade. And, to be fair, the night he planned for us sounds like a lot more fun than the thing I'm planning.

CHAPTER 9

We're experimenting with new cocktail concoctions when the doorbell rings. Luke goes to answer it while I taste test the whiskey and tequila mixed with cranberry juice and seltzer thing he just mixed for me. For the record, it's a miss.

I'm still wincing when he walks in with my brother and my best friend. "Not a winner?" he asks with a laugh, and I shake my head as I try to cleanse my palate with some plain seltzer, which tastes almost as bad as the Luke special he just had me try.

"It's a one-way route to Vomitsville," I say.

"Count me in," Josh jokes, and hugs are issued all around.

We end up with four simple whiskey and Cokes, all heavy on the whiskey, and the bell rings a few minutes later with our food delivery—a nice assortment of salads and fried appetizers. We take the food out to the back patio and sit under the pergola, which has landscape lights strung across the top and couches for us to relax on with a table in the middle where we set the food.

The sun has just set and the lights cast a romantic glow over the four of us. The air coolers I bought to try out ahead of our charity event are doing their thing, and so far, so good.

We fill each other in on everything we missed since the last time we saw each other (except, obviously, we leave out the dirty details about *all the sex* we've been having since, hello, this is my brother—but I *will* be filling Nicki in on the goods later).

Josh and Nicki are adjusting to life at home as newlyweds, which basically translates to mean that they haven't actually unpacked their bags yet because they've been so busy doing nothing (or maybe they're leaving out the dirty details for my benefit, too—for which I thank them. Profusely).

Luke and Josh head inside to refill our drinks, and that's when Nicki starts grilling me.

"You two are looking awfully cozy," she starts.

I grin. I can't help it. "It's like...God, it's like a dream come true."

"Give me every detail."

I giggle. "Some things shall remain between husband and wife."

"Liar. Is he a boob guy or an ass guy?"

"More boobs, but just because we haven't had a lot of time to really get to know one another yet."

"Josh is a total ass guy," she says.

"Nicki! There are things I don't need to know about my brother."

She laughs, and despite my horror, I do, too.

"Okay, boys aside, are you okay? Work going good? You're enjoying Vegas and staying forever?"

"That's a lot of questions," I say. "But, yeah, everything is going really well. I'm planning this charity thing and it's sucking up all my time. Invitations went out, so now I wait for the RSVPs and then I can really take off." I reach for another mozzarella stick. If there's one thing I can't resist besides glittery stickers, it's fried cheese.

"Consider the Nolans, party of two, there. This is our official RSVP. And tell me what I can do to help. I'm here for anything you need."

"You're the best," I say, munching on my fried goodness. "I will definitely take you up on that."

The boys rejoin us, and with more alcohol comes louder voices and more boisterous laughter. By the time they leave, it's well after midnight and I'm exhausted.

But not *too* exhausted.

"I'm gonna take a shower," Luke says as we finish cleaning up the kitchen.

"Care for some company?" I ask with a raised brow.

He takes a step toward me. "If you're offering, that's a definite yes." He pulls me into his arms.

"Oh, I'm offering. I've been waiting all night for them to leave so I could have some naked time with you." I lean forward and kiss him, and he chuckles before he sweeps me up into his arms and carries me up the stairs.

He sets me down once we arrive in the bathroom and he moves away from me only to turn on the water in the shower to let it warm up. He moves back into my orbit after he peels off his shirt and tosses it to the ground.

I peel mine off, too, tossing it somewhere near his.

He lowers his pants, and I mirror him.

We stand in our underwear, which we both remove next as we eye the other hungrily, and then he pounces. His mouth crashes down to mine as he pulls me against his rock hard body. This kiss is urgent and needy, all the pent-up desire from being apart for much of the day rising to the surface.

I've always loved the *honeymoon* phase of a relationship—that time when you just can't get enough of the other one, when it's all sex all the time and it's hot and fiery. But this is an *actual* honeymoon phase...and I find myself not wanting to ever move out of it as I kiss him back with all the same desire and passion he's giving me.

I know that's not possible. Work is starting up again for him very soon, and we'll have to face a new reality. And so I plan to indulge in every spare moment I possibly can in the meantime.

He moves us into the shower, a stream of hot water beating down on each of us thanks to dual shower heads, and our kiss turns slippery despite the urgency still there. He turns me around, and I reach for the glass of the side of the shower to brace myself as I bend forward to allow him the access he wants. He plunges into me then reaches around to grab my breasts in his hands. I claw at the glass as he pounds away at me. I need something to hold onto, something to grasp as the pleasure drives me closer and closer to the edge, but my hands simply slip on the wet glass. He paws at my breasts, and then he moves one of his hands down to brush against my clit while he continues to drive into me.

And then the flash of white light hits me, and I dive over the cliff into the abyss of bliss, my body contracting over his as his grunts turn into growls. A loud and sexy groan rips from his chest, and then he shoves into me a few more times as he lets go, too.

He slips out of me, and then he soaps my loofah and washes my body. I do the same for him, spending extra time massaging shampoo into his hair and stealing kisses around the stream of water.

He dries me off with tender care, kissing my body all over as he dries each spot, and then we collapse together into bed.

If this isn't sheer perfection, I'm not sure what is. I send up a prayer before I fall asleep that this feeling, this love, and this bond between us will last forever.

CHAPTER 10

I point to the giant white tent on the left. "That's the hospitality tent," I say, and the line of workers holding trays of food disperses in that direction.

I fold my arms over my chest and survey my work.

In the last three weeks, I've slept very little as I've worked my ass off to get this event off the ground. We're scheduled to have twenty-seven members of the Vegas Aces in attendance, eight other football players, a bunch of Aces staff—including the team owner—and, of course, Luke's brother, and most attendees are bringing dates or even entire families with them. I ended up reserving three huge tents and a few smaller ones, too. One of the big tents is filled with sand boxes and toys and smaller versions of the adult cornhole games set up to entertain the kids. We also have two bounce houses—one for kids four and under, the other for kids five and over. The hospitality tent has tables and chairs along with food served buffet style and drinks, and the third large tent is where the tournament will take place.

The smaller tents are the places where cornhole players will register and donations will be taken. The park has bathrooms, so I didn't even have to worry about that part of throwing a party.

Air coolers are set up in each of the tents, and while it's going to reach a blazing hot one hundred six degrees today, the coolers are definitely helping. I'd briefly considered having this event at Luke's house—*our* house—but decided this park was way better. A huge playground sits not too far away from us, and on the other side of the park is a splash pad to cool off the kids. It's a perfect example of the types of things Luke wants to build with the money he raises today.

And it all starts in less than an hour.

I draw in a deep breath as I look around.

I've done all I can do at this point. I've delegated every task I could think of to delegate, including hiring an official event photographer—but I'm still going to focus on taking pictures of Luke. I need as much footage as I can to show the community how much they need him here in Vegas.

Luke is in the tournament tent working with the men we hired to serve as our referees. Josh is with him, and Nicki is in the hospitality tent helping out there. I check on everybody, make sure nobody needs anything, and then I glance up and see the first of our guests as they start to arrive.

This is really happening.

My heart races.

I head to the hospitality tent for a cold bottle of water. It's showtime.

I grab Luke and the two of us walk toward the registration desk hand-in-hand to greet Luke's celebrity friends as they enter the First Annual Dalton Celebrity Cornhole Tournament to benefit the Luke and Ellie Dalton Foundation.

That's right. The Luke *and Ellie* Dalton Foundation.

That's what he wanted to name it. He said it wouldn't exist without my idea or the contributions I've made, and he thought it was important for my name to appear on the marquee.

I was too excited to turn him down, but what happens in a year from now when our *contract* is up? What if my last name isn't Dalton anymore?

I guess we'll cross that bridge when we get to it.

"Hey, Fletch," he says to the guy I recognize as Brandon Fletcher, the quarterback I met at the ball we attended together. A different woman is on his arm, dressed in freaking jeans and heels when we're at an outdoor tournament in a park. For my own part, I'm wearing a Dalton shirt, shorts, and sneakers. It's what Luke wanted, and he's in shorts and a t-shirt, too. We're comfortable, as opposed to the last charity event we attended together.

Luke introduces me as his wife to his teammates, and it's absolutely surreal that I'm even here right now. I recognize Nadine, Krista, and Leah, the football wives who were Nicki's bridesmaids, when they come in with their football player husbands.

When I spot Calvin as he makes his way toward the registration table, the woman on his arm surely can't be Michelle's mother. She might not even be as old as Michelle, to be honest.

I push the negative, judgmental thoughts away. It's not my place to judge someone else's relationship.

It just seems a little hypocritical that he expects Luke to give up his own happiness to be with Michelle when Cal himself is with someone who's not the mother of his own children (but who is probably in the same age range as his own children).

I'm sure they're desperately in love. I'm sure it has nothing to do with his money.

"Mr. Bennett!" Luke says brightly when Calvin gets to the front of the line. "We're so pleased you could make it."

Too much brightness, Luke. Dial it down a notch. We're not *that* happy he's here.

"This looks to be an incredible event. We're always thrilled to do our part to help the community. Isn't that right, darling?" he says to his date.

"Yes, of course," she says.

"Ensuring every kid has a fair shot to play sports is important to me," Luke says.

Calvin gives him an unreadable glance. "As long as your own kids come first," he murmurs, taking a bit of a shot.

"Of course," Luke says simply, and speak of the damn devil, up walk Jack and his date.

I blow out a breath as I recognize the woman on his arm. Michelle.

"You might've chosen a hotter day for this," Jack says in lieu of a hello, and the criticism isn't lost on me. God, I hope Luke hits him in the balls with a beanbag.

Sort of like I did to Luke on accident that time.

"Daddy!" Michelle says, rushing up to Calvin and throwing her arms around him.

"Shelly," he says affectionately, patting her on the back as she clings to him. "Have you been taking your vitamins?" he asks.

"Of course, Daddy," she says, and the sweet factor is beyond fake as she glances over at Luke to gauge his reaction to her even being here. "And I have an appointment this week. Jack said he'd come with me since he'll still be in town. Isn't that so sweet of him?"

Calvin purses his lips. "So Jack, the brother of the father, will be there? What about the actual father?" He glances in Luke's direction.

"Of course I'll be there," he says quickly. "In fact, both Ellie and I are thrilled to go." He grabs my hand.

I knew nothing about this appointment, but I nod and fake my way through it just like everyone else in this conversation seems to be doing. "We just need Michelle to fill us in on the exact time, date, and location." I smile sweetly, and then I completely change the subject. "Thank you all again for being here. We're so excited to raise money for this very important cause." It's my way of ushering them through the line.

And then, as if these people showing up at the same time wasn't enough, Savannah makes her way toward the table.

Why the hell did I think it was a good idea to invite them?

CHAPTER 11

To my extreme surprise, Savannah remains professional through the entire tournament, but I can't help wondering the whole time what, exactly, she has on the Dalton brothers and if I'll ever find out the truth. She basically ignores me, which is fine, and she takes notes throughout the day, which tells me that maybe she'll write an article about the event. I hope she does because any exposure for the foundation is good exposure.

The accountant we hired gives me the final number as the tournament draws to a close. Luke beat his brother, which made my heart absolutely sing (and his, too, I'm sure), but the final big winner of the tournament who will take home the trophy is Jaxon Bryant, star running back of the Vegas Aces.

I give the number to Luke, who takes the microphone the announcers had been using all day during the tournament. "Thank you to everyone who came today, to all the players who paid to be part of this tournament, to everyone who donated their time and money. I'm amazed at what a successful event this has been, but maybe I shouldn't be. After all, my new wife is the one who planned the entire thing while also planning a wedding. I'm proud to have her by my side," he says, nodding toward me and waving his hand in a *come up here* motion. He waits for me to join him on the stage before he continues. "Give it up for Ellie Dalton," he says, and I hear hoots and hollers at the mention of my name. I smile shyly as my cheeks color and I wave to the crowd assembled as they listen to Luke.

He turns back to the crowd. "Thanks to you and your generosity, we've managed to raise over one hundred thousand dollars. We'll continue taking donations today, so that number may still change. Thank you again. We hope you had a great time. I know I did, and if Ellie is up for it, we'll have another one of these tournaments next year. But maybe in, say, February."

That garners a laugh from the sweating crowd.

"Go Aces!" he yells, and his teammates all echo his sentiment with one loud baritone *Go Aces!*

And then it's all over. People say their goodbyes and start making their way back to their cars.

For all the planning that went into this event, as quickly as it began...here we are at the end. We're married. Our charity event is over. Training camp starts next week.

Now what?

I've been running around settling tabs with vendors, and Luke has been a gracious host as he talks to groups of people before they take off. Nicki and Josh are still around helping out, too. So I'm surprised when I see Jack and Michelle still sitting in the hospitality tent as everyone else except Luke, me, Nicki, and Josh has cleared out.

Michelle is talking and Jack looks bored beside her. People move all around them taking down tables and chairs, but they seem oblivious.

And then I watch Jack as his eyes zero in on his brother, who sits alone in the registration tent as he glances through the notebook where the volunteers kept track of donations. Minus the expenses from today, we made a huge chunk of money that will go directly back to the community.

I don't like that they're still here, but at least they didn't cause any problems during the actual event. I head toward Luke to see if he needs any help.

"You know your brother is still here?" I ask him when I get to the tent.

He glances up at the sound of my voice. "Ellie, this is incredible. It far exceeded any of my expectations." He stands and presses a kiss to my cheek. "*You* are incredible. Thank you for the idea, for the event, for being here for me."

One of the papers on the table is swept up in a random gust of wind and flies just outside the tent. "I'll grab it," I say.

It flutters away from me to the backside of the tent, and as I bend to pick it up, I hear another voice join Luke's.

"What do you want?" Luke asks.

"Just hear me out," Jack says. There's a pause, and then Jack says, "I'll triple my donation if you divorce her."

Why would he want us divorced? Why does he care so much about making sure I'm not in Luke's life?

There's another brief pause, and I can't see either of them from where I'm frozen on the other side of the tent, but I still so as not to make a sound. I imagine in that brief pause, Luke does something to indicate they aren't alone. "Forget it. I love Ellie, and I don't need your damn donation. And by the way, you can stop blackmailing me now. I have as much on you as you have on me."

Jack blows out a frustrated breath. "You can't tell her. This stays between you, me, and Savannah. You know it could ruin both our careers if it gets out. Her brother is on the Aces, man." His words clearly show that he didn't get it if Luke was trying to warn him that I'm standing right here overhearing this entire conversation.

"And, may I remind you, you're showing up everywhere lately with my team owner's daughter," Luke says.

"Yeah, we're so in love." The sarcasm isn't lost on me, and I get the sudden feeling the only reason Jack has been hanging around her is so he has something he can hold over Luke...but Luke doesn't really care *who* Michelle hangs out with as long as it isn't us.

"Look, we both have a lot to lose if anyone finds out," Luke says, his voice low like he's trying to be quiet enough for me not to overhear since he knows I'm standing right here. "Ellie is my wife now. I trust her with my life. Look at what she did for me today."

My heart balloons in my chest. I hate Jack a little more now, but I also get that he's trying to protect whatever secret they all have.

It seems like it's a secret they're holding pretty tightly onto...but secrets always have a way of coming out.

I slowly walk across the field toward Nicki, who watches me as I walk. "Were you just spying on the brothers Dalton?"

I shake my head. "No. I was grabbing this piece of paper when Jack walked up and they started talking. I just don't want Jack to ruin what has been such a great day for Luke."

"Why'd you invite him, then?"

I make a face. "His fat checkbook."

She laughs, but I'm not laughing. I want to tell someone what I just overheard...but clearly this is a secret they want to keep. If I mention it to Nicki, then I'll just have added pressure to find it out.

No...I better not say anything. But I might just have to ask Luke later.

Especially if this could affect the careers of these brothers. I'm his publicist now. If making him look indispensable to the team is part of my job, I need to know what skeletons are hiding in his closets so I'm equipped to handle them when they jump out.

CHAPTER 12

I glance at the picture on the wall above Michelle's head.

Four little tiny baby fingers wrapped around a single adult finger, and the thumb coming around the other side. Precious.

I knew my "husband" had gotten another woman pregnant, but I didn't really think about what that meant until this very moment. I know nothing about kids, but once Michelle has this baby, I'm going to have to learn. I'll be a stepmother of sorts to this child.

Part of me even wonders if Luke is going to ask Michelle to move in so he can be close to the baby. He's just the kind of guy who would do exactly that even if it's the last thing he— or his wife—personally wants.

It's weird sitting here, Luke's hand in mine and Michelle sitting across from us and next to Jack. I shouldn't even be here, really, and neither should Jack.

I've always wanted kids, but I assumed they'd be a little further into my future. And, if I'm being honest, I assumed they'd be *mine*, too. I assumed I'd be the mother, not the woman married to the father-to-be.

As we sit here, I sort of start to see the reality of why Luke felt so desperate that the only answer he could see was to marry another woman.

"Michelle?" a woman calls, and the four of us stand. The woman looks surprised as she sees the two lean, attractive men walking toward the ultrasound room with Michelle and me. "Last name?" she asks.

"Bennett," Michelle says.

"Right through here," she says with a smile, and the four of us follow her to the room.

Michelle sits on a table, Jack takes the chair beside her, and Luke and I hang back. The ultrasound technician turns off the lights. "Lie back, lift your shirt, and lower your pants just a little," she says. Michelle does, and she squirts some gel onto Michelle's stomach. She moves it around with a wand, and we all see some movement on the large television screen broadcasting Michelle's uterus. There's a bunch of other information on there, too. Dates and codes and things I assume are in some way related to pregnancy but I have no actual idea.

"There's baby," the tech says, and I strain to see what she's talking about. I really just see some wavy white lines on a black backdrop.

"Where?" Luke asks, voicing my own question.

She takes a mouse and points to the baby on the screen. She circles a blob. "Right here," she says.

"Can you tell if it's a boy or a girl?" Luke asks.

"Not yet with certainty on the ultrasound, but if Michelle had the genetic testing done at ten weeks, the doctor should be able to tell you if you want to know," the tech says. She doesn't leave room for questions—like the one I have, which is whether Michelle already knows if it's a boy or a girl. "I'm just going to take a few measurements. Michelle, you'll feel some pressure, okay?"

"Okay," she says, and it's so weird that we're all looking at the baby chilling in her uterus as the tech moves the wand all around.

Once the tech is done, she hands over a printout of the session. "You can head back to the lobby and the doctor will call you back shortly for your exam."

"Does everything look okay?" Luke asks.

"Growth is on track and the baby looks healthy," the tech says with a smile.

"Thanks," Luke says.

The four of us head back toward the lobby.

"Do you know the gender?" Luke asks.

Michelle shakes her head.

"I want to know," he says.

"Okay. I don't."

"Then I won't tell you," he says thickly. "But I have a right to know."

Michelle just huffs in reply, and it may be kind of a petty argument, but it does give me some insight into why they ended things. They're just not compatible, and if they argue on things like finding out gender, certainly they'll argue over the bigger issues later.

My heart aches for Luke. He wasn't expecting this twist of fate, and he certainly doesn't want to share a kid with this woman he thought he'd written out of his life story, and now because of one drunken night, he's stuck with her forever.

"Michelle?" Luke asks.

"Hmm?" she asks, lazily playing with Jack's hand as she clutches it.

"Why did the chart in there put your date of conception at March thirty-first?"

Michelle blinks in Luke's direction. "Huh?"

"The date of conception," Luke repeats. "We weren't together March thirty-first. We weren't together until that weekend. April fifth."

My heart races.

If what he's saying is true...what if he's not the father?

It crossed my mind when we first found out, but Michelle said he is, and he admitted they had a night, so we all assumed she was telling the truth.

But what if she isn't?

Between the wedding and the charity event plus working on Luke's public image, I sort of let the whole idea of whether Luke is really this baby's father go. But maybe it's time to revisit that train of thought.

"That's an estimate based on the date of my last period. If you want more details, I'd be happy to get them for you. You know, like the length of my periods, how many tampons I go through..."

Luke holds up a hand. "I don't think that's necessary."

A paternity test might be, though.

I don't bring it up in the lobby of the obstetrician's office, obviously.

No...I wait until Luke and I are home, long after Michelle and Jack have slithered off to wherever it is they go. Sheila just left after doing a deep clean of the whole house, Pepper is taking a nap in the family room, and we're enjoying some of Debbie's homemade shredded chicken tacos for dinner.

"So you think it's yours?" I blurt.

Luke chuckles. "I wish I could say I have no reason to believe it isn't...but I don't trust Michelle."

"You mentioned you have some experience with paternity tests. Care to share more about that?"

He blows out a breath and takes a bite of taco before he answers. "I've had two women allege I was the father of their unborn children. For the record, I have no children. I was stupid, but I always wore condoms unless I was in a relationship. I know they're not a hundred percent, but I requested both women take a paternity test anyway."

"And they came back negative?"

He chuckles. "Something like that. They came back and showed I was not a match to the child."

"Can they do one of those when she's pregnant?"

He nods. "They can do a blood draw and compare DNA that way. It's completely safe for both mother and child."

"Then do it. Make her take one," I say.

"It's not that simple," he says. "Aside from the fact that her father would murder me if he thought I was indicating that baby isn't mine, she claims she wasn't with anyone else. She's sure it's mine. And besides, we'd been in a relationship. I wasn't exactly running for the condom box. I never found a condom in the morning, so we can both guess what that means."

"You're assuming you had sex," I point out. I want to eat my taco because it's so damn delicious, but I also need answers. "What if you didn't? Drunk Luke hates Michelle just as much as sober Luke."

"I can't deny that."

"You don't even have definitive proof that you slept with her. Why aren't you putting up a little more of a fight here?"

He stares down at his plate. "She says it's mine. Her father has the ability to take away everything that matters to me. What choice do I have, Ellie?"

I don't have an answer for that. He's right. He's stuck.

"Have you thought about asking her for proof it's yours?" I ask.

"Of course I have. But then I think about how her father would react to that if he ever found out, and something stops me."

"There isn't anything stopping *me*," I say, suggesting I'm happy to do his dirty work for him.

He looks thoughtfully at me for a beat. "I guess I can't really stop you if I don't know anything about it."

"I'm your wife, Luke," I say. "I'm here to protect you, to fight for you, to fight *with* you. We'll get to the truth no matter what it takes."

His eyes lock on mine across the table, and he nods briefly. "Thank you." His voice is soft and sincere and full of emotion.

"Don't thank me until we have our answers."

But I *will* get those answers.

Whatever it takes.

CHAPTER 13

I sit in the backyard with Pepper the next Monday morning. I stare at the empty treadmill that's sadly not getting any use now that Luke is away at training camp.

The Aces rent out some vineyard in California for the first two weeks of camp before coming back home to have the rest of camp at their practice facility. Their first preseason game is mid-August, a few days after they return home from the vineyard.

It sounds like a vacation, but Luke has assured me that it's not. Instead, his days are filled with workouts and practices and new formations and schemes and battles for position. Nights are filled with recovery, and early mornings are filled with cryotherapy and massages.

Still sounds like a vacation to me.

Josh is gone, too, and Nicki and I have already talked at length about how we'll spend every waking moment together. Except I'm awake right now and Nicki's not here, so I guess that promise was a bit of an exaggeration.

I post a picture of Luke and a story with a picture he sent me last night of the vineyard where he's staying. I do some research on how players contribute to the community even when they're in season.

And then, on a total whim, I take a quick glance at local public relations agencies. I need something to do. Handling one client isn't enough to fill my days, especially now that our little charity event is over and he's not even here to create thirst traps I can snap pictures of.

I have nothing on the horizon. In short, I'm bored.

I step onto the treadmill. I think about the hot guy who usually uses it. I click some buttons, but it's useless. I can't even get the damn thing to turn on. So instead, I take a walk around the yard. I toss the ball for Pepper, but she gets bored with me after a few runs across the yard.

This is just the first day of this new reality. I need to get out. I need to find a hobby. I need *something*.

The doorbell rings a little before eleven, and when I open it, I find Debbie standing on the other side with bags of groceries.

"Hey Debbie!" I say probably with way too much enthusiasm. "What are you doing here?" I take the bags from her and she follows me into the kitchen. I figured without Luke here, she'd take a couple weeks off.

"Oh, dear, you still need your nourishment. I'll be making your favorites." She winks at me. "Or, at least, the things Luke told me were your favorites."

"You don't have to do all this. You should take this time off while Luke's away." I don't mind cooking, anyway. In fact, I sort of like it...plus it gives me something to pass the time.

"I don't mind. It gives me something to do." She smiles at me, and suddenly I feel a little bond with her. She may have lost her husband when he passed away, which is very different from what I'm feeling, but we're both searching for a purpose. She found hers when she started cooking for Luke.

I have yet to find mine. Maybe I'll look through those local agencies again.

Debbie and I chat while she gets started making the shredded chicken for the tacos—definitely one of my favorites—and it's nearly four in the afternoon by the time she's done and takes off. I text Nicki.

Me: *What are you up to? I'm bored.*

Nicki: *Reorganizing my kitchen. Want to come help?*

Not even a little bit.

Me: *Sure. Be right over.*

"Do you think the plates should go in this cabinet?" Nicki points to one. "Or this one?" She points to another one.

I don't care.

I don't say that, obviously. This is my best friend. But I don't even like organizing my *own* kitchen, let alone someone else's. When I moved into Luke's place and it was already done, I was good to go. As Nicki should have been. She's lived in this house for over a year. Who takes literally everything out of their cabinets only to change which one the plates are stored in after a year of habitually going to the same cabinet?

"That one," I say, pointing to the first one. "It's closest to the oven, which will be convenient for plating your food." Like she ever cooks.

Okay, I'm being snarky. I need to work on that.

"So give me the real talk. What's it like being married to a football player?" I ask, setting down the bowl in my hand to have a conversation with Nicki.

She sets down the wineglass she's polishing and slides onto the stool next to me. "It's wonderful and frustrating and awful and amazing all at once."

"What's a typical game week like?" I ask, setting my chin in my palm as I lean on the counter.

"If they win on Sunday, they get Monday off. Sort of. Coaches will email film for them to study but they don't have to go in. If they lose on Sunday, they go in on Monday. Tuesday is their day off, so it's the one day when they can connect with the community or do rehab if they need to, but it's also the one day they get with you. Wednesday is technique practice and Thursday is strategy practice for the upcoming game. They go hard and intense. Friday is a travel day if it's an away game, and they do light situational practice or strategy meetings when they get wherever they're going. Saturday is a light practice at the stadium and Saturday night they stay in a hotel."

"For away games, right?" I ask.

She shakes her head and picks up the wineglass. "Home or away."

My brows dip. "They stay in a hotel the night before a game even if they're playing at home?"

"Yep." She stands and picks up another wineglass that apparently needs polishing. "They have a curfew to make sure they get enough sleep and are ready to play on Sunday regardless of which city they're in. Every team is a little different, but the Aces do bed checks on Friday nights, too, if they're out of town. I guess Fridays used to be crazy party nights whenever they'd travel somewhere away from home, but Coach Thompson put a stop to that."

"That's crazy. They don't even get to go out?" I ask. "These are grown men."

"Right. And they're getting huge paychecks to play a game. The Aces just want to make sure their players are ready to do what they're being paid to do."

"Don't some of the guys resent that?"

"Thompson is great about spinning it to make it come from a place of caring about each player rather than keeping tabs on them. The younger guys don't always get it at first, but guys have been kicked off the team for repeatedly missing curfew. They take it pretty seriously when they know their job's at stake."

"Wow. Serious business."

She nods. "The Aces are great in the way they take care of their guys. You'll see."

"Fingers crossed," I murmur. I'm still more than a little worried about Luke's future with the team given the owner's feelings toward him.

I'm surrounded by plates and bowls when my phone dings with a new text. I grab it out of my pocket with the hope that whatever this message says will get me out of actually having to put all this shit away.

Luke: *We're free for the next half hour if you're around to talk.*

I glance up and see Nicki reading a text on her phone, too. This must be the official *call your wife* time.

"I'm gonna call Josh," Nicki says.

"I'm going to head home. It's Pepper's dinner time anyway and I just got a text from Luke, too."

She gives me a quick hug. "You can come back here for dinner if you want. I'm ordering Chinese."

"Thanks, but Debbie left me chicken tacos. You're welcome to join me."

She glances around her kitchen and sighs. "Thanks, but I've got a project I can't give up on now."

I laugh. "Check in tomorrow, okay?"

She nods. "I'm actually getting together with the other football wives tomorrow for lunch. Come with me. You're one of us now."

I nod. "Okay. That sounds fun, actually." Not only will it give me something to do, but it actually *does* sound fun. It's time I get to know some people in the area—even if it's not the best idea to get attached to the football wife lifestyle.

I call Luke as soon as I walk in the front door.

"Hey," he answers softly, and his warm voice sounds exhausted.

"How's the first day?" I ask.

"Reminding me why the average age in the league is twenty-six."

I chuckle. "You okay?"

"Let's just say I'm looking forward to the cryotherapy in the morning."

"What exactly is that?" I ask. "You've mentioned it a few times."

"It's cold therapy. I stand in a chamber in freezing temps for three minutes."

I make a face even though he can't see it. "That sounds awful."

He laughs. "It helps with muscle pain. It's worth the three minutes of freezing my ass off for the benefits."

"So what was today like that you're already in pain?"

"It's the first day. Everyone pushes hard to show they didn't fuck around in the offseason. The rookies are trying to prove themselves—well, the ones who don't walk around like they know everything, anyway. And the old guys—that's me—are trying to prove they're still relevant."

"You're still relevant," I say softly.

He sighs. "I like to think so."

"Does the owner go to camp?"

"Not this leg of it," he says. "He'll be there when we're back home, but he doesn't come out here. This is just coaches and players. It gives us a little time to get back into things, to get to know the new guys, and to get back in shape."

"And to use the cold chamber."

"We have a chamber at our practice facility, too," he says. "Out here, they have four. We only have one, and the line tends to get lengthy waiting for it."

"What does a vineyard need four cold chambers for?" I ask.

"Aside from actually freezing grapes, we're not the only guests who frequent this facility. There's a whole therapy wing that gets used pretty much year-round by different athletes."

"Interesting. So what's next on the agenda?"

"Dinner in, well, fifteen minutes now, and then we have meetings with our position coaches. What have you been up to today?" he asks.

"Trying to find something to do. Pepper has been well-exercised and I've realized how entertaining you must be."

He chuckles. "You know, a few guys mentioned to me how impressed they are with my social media presence."

"They did?"

"Yep," he says. "I actually had two who asked me if my publicist is taking on more clients. If you're interested, I'm sure I could rally up more than just two guys. As long as I always come first."

"Seriously?" I'm in awe. I just wanted to help the guy who offered me a place to stay, and now I'm working for him, married to him, and he's pimping me out—in a good, professional way, of course. "What did you tell the ones who asked about me?"

"That I'd talk to you about it. I know you said you don't know enough about athletes to take them on as clients, but from what I'm hearing...that doesn't really matter. You'll research what you don't know, but what you know about PR more than makes up for what you don't know when it comes to the game. So I guess...just think about it."

"I will," I promise...even though it's a no-brainer. Of course I'll take on more clients. He's right. I'll research what I don't know. Are there people better equipped to take on athletes as clients? Absolutely. But I don't know all that much about architecture, and one of my clients was a firm in Chicago. I don't know that much about lingerie, but I learned when I had to work with Todd on a client who needed a total rebrand after a celebrity was caught gifting their goods to a hooker.

And I'll learn more about football, too.

Especially since it'll help make Luke even more indispensable to the Aces, which is my end-goal in the first place.

CHAPTER 14

Leah, Nadine, and Krista are already sitting at a round table when Nicki and I walk into the restaurant.

"I hear congratulations are in order," Nadine says to me, and I grin widely and flash my hand so everyone can check out my sparkly new hardware.

"Good catch," Leah says. "So many women have tried to tie that one down—including Calvin's daughter. How'd you manage to do it? And so quickly?"

I shrug, trying not to feel defeated that Michelle has already been brought up as I slide into an open chair and Nicki takes the one beside me. "We've known each other a while through Josh. The timing was just right, I guess."

"Didn't you just break up with someone?" Krista asks, and I get the feeling she doesn't believe what Luke and I have is real.

"Yep. But when the timing is right with Luke Dalton, you jump at the chance. Am I right?" I get a laugh out of most of the ladies gathered. Not Krista.

"Well congrats, girl," Nadine says. "But now you'll be a one-night stand virgin forever."

Everyone shares a laugh, and I don't correct her. Because I'm not anymore. Not really.

"So tell me everything I need to know about being a football wife," I say, trying to push the spotlight off me and allow these ladies to shine.

Leah launches into the same warnings she gave Nicki about lifting your husband up so some other woman doesn't swoop in, Nadine talks about how important it is to maintain my own identity and have things that are just for me, and Krista tells me who I need to get to know in the staff offices. Apparently there are tons of activities for the wives and families of players, things like ladies' luncheons, community events, charity work, and even Bible study groups if I'm so inclined to be part of any of it.

And I am inclined. I don't just need something to fill the hours...I need a community. But does it make sense for me to become a part of this community only to have to leave it in a year?

I'm scared to form attachments that I won't get to keep. And nothing says I won't still be around in a year. We can stay together forever if that's what we decide, but the contract only stipulates a year.

Even so, it makes sense to immerse myself in this experience. Getting involved and helping anywhere I can, being supportive of my husband—these seem like more ways to prove that this team needs Luke.

"Richard mentioned you've taken over Luke's social media," Nadine says. "How's that going?"

"He hired me as his publicist. I used to do public relations back in Chicago and when we talked about his total lack of media and community presence, I said I'd take him on," I explain.

"What's it like working with your husband?" Krista asks.

I raise a brow. "Have you seen the thirst traps I've posted? It's not hard."

The girls laugh. "Well you've done wonders," Nadine says. "People are taking notice, and not just the social media stuff, but the community outreach. Can you take on Richard, too?" she asks.

I chuckle. "For the right price."

Nadine laughs and winks at Nicki. "I like her."

My chest warms at the thought of building a bond with these women. We sit chatting for hours even after we've all finished our lunches. We sip wine and laugh, and I'm already starting to get that first feeling like I'm a part of something.

I learn that these two weeks are the loneliest of the entire season because even when the guys have to travel for games, they're usually only gone Friday through Sunday.

Leah invites me to go with her to the staff offices tomorrow so she can introduce me to all the key people, and I jump at the chance. Not only will it seal my own place as a football wife, but it's also giving me the chance to get to know Leah. I could certainly do with more friends out here in Vegas since my old ones basically ditched me when I left Chicago.

I think of Brittany. She was my best friend at the office back home, and when she got wind of my tryst with Todd and the way we were both fired, she faded immediately away. If that taught me anything, it's that scandals prove who your true friends are.

I've learned my only true friend is Nicki. She's the only one who has been by my side since we were teenagers, and now she's family. But I'm working on a complete transformation. Maybe it's okay to make some new friends—especially if these are people Nicki trusts.

* * *

"This is Erin," Leah says, stopping in a doorway. "She's the director of charitable contributions. Erin, this is Ellie Dalton, Luke's new wife."

Erin glances up and smiles.

"We've met," I say, smiling at Erin. "Good to see you again. Thanks for all your advice with our event. It went amazingly well."

"I saw Savannah's story in the *Sun*. Great work, Ellie. I never would've imagined it was the first event you organized based on its success."

"Thank you," I say, feeling a little self-conscious at her compliment. "I couldn't have done it without your help."

We move to the next office. "This is Phil, Director of Player Engagement and Development," Leah says. "Phil, meet Ellie, Luke Dalton's new wife."

"Ellie," Phil says warmly as he stands. He sticks his hand out over his desk to shake mine. "Nice to meet you."

"And you," I say. I'm about to ask what, exactly, his job entails when he beats me to the punch.

"I'm here to help players set career goals both while they're with the organization and with what comes after," he explains.

"Oh, yes." I nod. "You and I need to schedule a meeting about what comes next for Luke."

He chuckles. "I've been trying to get that guy to commit to some sort of goal regarding what comes next for *years*. Here's to hoping you have better luck than me."

I press my lips together. "That definitely sounds like my husband."

Leah introduces me to Terry, the Director of Community Relations, and a few other key people. The name plate on the last office we get to says *Monique Thompson*.

"Thompson?" I ask.

Leah nods. "Maybe the most important person you'll need to know in this entire organization...Coach's wife." Leah knocks on the door, and we hear a *come in* a second later. I'm suddenly a little nervous.

"Leah!" the elegant woman behind the desk says. I'd pin her at mid-fifties, but despite the elegance, she has this motherly aura about her. She stands and moves around to give her a hug. "And you must be Ellie," she says to me. She pulls me into a hug, and somehow she's warm and comforting and at the same time gorgeous and stylish in her dress and heels. "I'm Mo, but you can call me *mom* or *Mama Mo*. All the other ladies do." She smiles as she pulls out of our hug. "Now look at you." She eyes me up and down, and then she grabs my hand and ogles my wedding ring. "The one who finally tied down Mr. Luke Dalton. Good work, girl. Make it stick."

God, how I hope I can. Michelle edges into my mind at that moment. She's one of the ones who *tried* to tie down the man I married.

I wonder what Mo's opinion on her is. I know what *mine* is. Was she as friendly to the boss's daughter as she's being to me? Did Michelle get special treatment...or was she even a part of this club? And what happens now that she's not with Luke anymore? Does she just get voted off the island or something?

These might be questions best suited for Nicki.

"You two sit," she says, and we do as she makes her way around her desk. "I'm so glad Leah brought you by. You know, when she and Dave were engaged, it was Nadine who brought her by to introduce me to her, and I love how the torch is being passed." She folds her hands in front of her on top of the desk. "Welcome, welcome, welcome. I'm here for *anything* you need, whether it's a shoulder to cry on because you and Luke got into a fight all the way to a recommendation for where to go when your claws need a pedi."

I giggle at her description.

"I'm the president of the Ace of Hearts Club for the wives and girlfriends of players. You're the newest member of this very exclusive, very private, and very fun club, one that brings a ton of blessings but also a few curses. We're all here for you, and in fact I'm planning a luncheon for next Wednesday. Come. I'll introduce you and you can dive right into whatever you're interested in."

"Thank you," I say. "I appreciate it."

"Do you know many people here in town aside from your brother and Nicki?" she asks, and I love how she already knows this. It makes me feel even more a part of this club she's referring to.

I shake my head. "I met Leah, Nadine, and Krista through Nicki, but that's it. I'm completely new to town."

"Well you've got me now, and all the other ladies. They're just going to love you. And they'll all be banging your door down to take thirst traps of their men. Not for public consumption...just for their own." She winks, and I laugh.

"Luke isn't exactly a tough subject to photograph," I admit.

She laughs. "I don't think you'll get any arguments there."

We chat a little longer before we say our goodbyes, and on my way out the door, she hands me a folder. "All the important contact information you need is in there. Don't hesitate to text me or call me any time of the day or night. Supporting the wives is what I'm here to do." She gives me another hug, and I love her. I love this organization. I love my husband. I love the place I'm settling into here.

I just hope I get to keep it all.

CHAPTER 15

The day has been too good, and I feel that deep in my bones as we make our way toward the exit. My chest is warm and I feel like I've found a place where I belong even though I have no idea how long it'll last.

Does anyone, though?

Players can be traded or fall to a career-ending injury at any time. Separation and divorce run rampant for any marriage, but ones in the spotlight come with different sorts of pressures and complications.

So I'm claiming my place here while I can.

But the day has been the sort of good where I feel something coming to blindside me, and sure enough, just before we get to the exit doors to seal in what I can only describe as a feeling that I'm home, I hear my name.

"Ellie?"

I turn around and blow out a breath. "Michelle."

"Were you here looking for me?" she asks.

I shake my head nicely as I try to act like that's not the most self-centered, egotistical question I've ever heard. "No," I say. "Leah was just introducing me to some of the office staff."

"You must've skipped by my office," she says pointedly.

"You work here?" I ask.

"I figured you two already knew one another," Leah says, a touch of defensiveness in her tone. The boss's daughter really sort of puts everybody on edge.

"Yes," Michelle says, answering my question and ignoring Leah. "I'm currently serving as the administrative assistant to the director of marketing."

"That's wonderful," I say sweetly when what I really want to say is something along the lines of how it must be nice that her daddy gave her a job. Didn't Luke say something about how she'd just gotten back from studying fashion overseas when they first met? Good to see she's putting her fashion experience to good use.

"I'm glad I ran into you," she says.

"You are?" I ask, and I brace myself for whatever she's about to say.

"I was going to swing by the house tomorrow so we could have a chat since I don't have your number."

"A chat about what?" What could the two of us possibly have to talk about?

"About me moving back in."

My brows practically fly off my forehead as my eyes widen.

"Oh," she forces a fake chuckle as she covers her mouth with her hands. "I'm so sorry. Did Luke not tell you? We talked last night and I'll be moving my stuff in this weekend."

I narrow my eyes at her. What's the right move? Is she lying and trying to trap me? I won't play that game. "Luke and I haven't discussed you moving back in. That's not something I'm comfortable with."

"Good thing your opinion doesn't really matter then." She wiggles her fingers at me and flashes me a smile over her shoulder as she turns to walk away. "I'll see you Friday."

"The fuck you will," I mutter to her retreating figure.

I need to have a little chat with my dear husband.

As we walk back out to Leah's car, she's quiet. Once we slide into our seats so she can drive me back home, she starts up the car and glances at me. "You want to talk about what just happened?" she asks.

I twist my hands in my lap. "I hate her."

Leah chuckles. "Tell me how you really feel."

"She's so manipulative. I don't even really believe the baby is Luke's, yet she's moving back in? Fuck that. I need a goddamn paternity test before I even consider letting her move in. And I need to talk to Luke." I barely know Leah, and I should be thinking about whether I can really trust her. She was one of Nicki's bridesmaids. If Nicki trusts her, I'm sure I can, too. Right?

But I have no idea what her relationship with Michelle is.

"But you can't until the little ten-minute window he gives you later tonight." Leah sighs heavily. "I hate training camp month."

The feeling is definitely mutual.

When my phone rings a little after eight, I immediately pick it up. "Hey there, hubby," I say.

He doesn't even muster a chuckle. "Hey."

That one syllable sort of puts me on alert. "What's wrong?"

"Rough day. I'm exhausted."

He doesn't exactly sound like he's in the mood to chat about Michelle, but I need to get this off my chest and find some answers. And I also need to know when, exactly, he made time to chat with her when he can barely fit *me* in. "I ran into Michelle today."

"You did?"

"Yeah. Leah was introducing me to the key people I need to know in the Aces organization and we happened to cross paths in the lobby. And isn't this fresh? She said you gave her the green light to move into our house."

"She said what?" he thunders.

"Yep. She's moving in this Friday. It'll be just the two of us. Isn't that sweet? Oh, and by the way, when did you have time to talk to her?"

He blows out a breath. "We talked last night," he confirms, and I fume.

I've been missing him like crazy. I get all of five minutes of his time each night...yet he somehow made time for *her*.

I blow out a breath. "You made time to talk to her when I barely get a second of your time?"

"She called from Calvin's line at the office. When your boss calls, you answer." He still sounds tired. "And I never said she could move in. I said we'd talk about the possibility."

"So why on Earth does she think she's moving in on Friday?" I demand.

He's quiet a beat, and then he mutters a curse. "I may have said something just to appease her."

"Such as?"

"That I'd talk to you about it. I figured we'd come up with a plan together, and then I had another meeting and to be honest I forgot about it. See? That's what she does. She waits until she *knows* she can manipulate me because I'm not in the right frame of mind."

"What, exactly, did you mean when you said you would talk to me about it?" I ask.

He sighs. "I told her that if you were okay with it, we'd figure something out. She must've taken that to mean that you *were* okay with it and it's fine for her to move in."

"I refuse to live with her until we have a positive paternity test, Luke." My voice is flat and unmistakably clear.

"I get that. It's fine. I'll call her right now and tell her no."

"Please do that. I know you're busy and this is the hardest couple weeks of the year for you, and I know she's your boss's daughter, but that does not give you a pass to let her manipulate *me*."

"Understood," he says. "I will fix this."

"Now. Bye." I hang up with shaking hands as anger fills me.

I realize too late that it isn't Luke I'm mad at. It's Michelle. And I just sent him off to call her, and she's going to lay it on thick and probably make him feel like he might lose his job over this, and it's all because I'm insecure.

She's winning. She's coming between us, and I'm letting her.

I have to find a way to play this game with her. I'm not quite sure what the rules are since she's making them up as she goes, but I guarantee one thing.

I'm going to find a way to beat her at her own game.

CHAPTER 16

I'm just finishing up some scrambled eggs for breakfast when the doorbell rings. I'm a little wary to actually answer it. What if it's Michelle?

Pepper beats me to the door, and when I open it, I see Greg standing there. Luke's lawyer. I only met him once when we had our contract drawn up.

"Hi," I say, my voice hesitant. "Luke isn't home..."

"I know," he says, smiling broadly. "I'm here to see you. And don't worry, I come with good news. God, lawyers hardly *ever* get to say that."

I open the door a little wider to allow him in. "Come on in."

We move to the kitchen since that's the epicenter of where guests hang out in a home, and he opens his briefcase. He slides some papers across the counter toward me.

"Luke believes in your abilities as a publicist so deeply that he wants to gift you your own company. Here I have the paperwork for you to create your own LLC, a business plan, and a check to cover start-up expenses."

My jaw hangs unattractively open. "Uh...what?"

Is this his way of apologizing for our fight last night?

Or was this already in the works? It had to have already been in the works. There's no way Greg could've shown up here that quickly since our fight was just over thirteen hours ago.

Greg chuckles. "You heard me correctly. Luke wants you to create your own agency. He has clients chomping at the bit, but you need a business plan first. And I realize you're a publicist, not a businessperson, so I'm here to answer questions and help you complete the paperwork. Luke wants this to be yours and solely yours." He clears his throat and lowers his voice. "It's something you can take with you at the culmination of your contract."

Oh.

And just like that, the wind is completely knocked from my sails at the reminder. I wonder if those are Greg's words or Luke's, and to be clear, the answer to that does make a difference. It would explain whether Luke still sees the end of our contract as the end of us.

He's giving me something wonderful, and I'm going to choose to focus on that. Those had to have been Greg's words.

"I can't believe he'd do all that for me."

He offers a small smile. "He cares about you, Ellie. Deeply." He seems like he wants to add more, but he doesn't. I wonder if that falls under the whole client confidentiality thing.

We spend the next several hours filling out paperwork. When it comes time to name the company, Greg throws out a bunch of suggestions. "Ellie Nolan Public Relations? Ellie Dalton? Dalton PR?"

"Prince Charming Public Relations," I say emphatically. "PCPR."

This may be my company, but it will always hold the name of the man who gifted it to me.

I just hope I don't live to regret that decision.

* * *

All day I've been waiting to hear from him. I wanted to call him to thank him for the gift, and with an apology for our fight, and with curiosity as to whether he got in touch with Michelle, but I forced myself to be patient so as not to bother him while he's working. I thought about sending a text message, but I want him to hear my genuine gratitude in my voice. So by the time my phone rings a little after eight, I grab it immediately.

"Thank you," I gush in lieu of a hello. "You are the most amazing man on the planet."

He chuckles. "I don't know about that."

"My very own Prince Charming," I say.

He laughs.

"Which is why I named it PCPR."

"PC...for Prince Charming?" he asks.

"Yep. I named it after you."

"Wow, Ellie," he says, a touch of surprise in his tone. "Thank you."

"Thank *you* for everything, Luke. I promise I won't let you down. This will be the most successful public relations company in all of Las Vegas."

"With you at the helm, I don't doubt that. And that reminds me, I have three potential new clients for you," he says. "I sent their information to Greg, and he'll forward it to you once he gets your official email set up. Knowing him, it'll be there by morning."

"I look forward to it. Thanks for talking me up to your buddies."

"I didn't have to. They saw what you did with the charity event. They were there. They see the benefit to what you're doing for me, and if they see it, Calvin will, too. And that's where this all started in the first place, right?" he asks.

"Yeah. That reminds me. The player relations guy...what's his name again?" I ask.

"Phil?"

"Yes, Phil. He said he's been trying to get you to set some post-playing goals for years now," I say.

He laughs. "Yeah, but remember what I said in Hawaii? It's bad luck to talk about the future."

I roll my eyes. "Yeah, yeah."

"Oh, and I called Michelle last night but she didn't answer. I'm still working on straightening that one out."

I sigh. "I thought about it a lot last night, Luke, and I'm starting to think she's doing all this on purpose. She's working hard to come between us. What if we just let her move in? Let her see firsthand that this is real, that we're in love, that she can pick and pry all she wants but it won't matter because we're married now?"

"I think that's a terrible idea," he says.

"I do, too, but what if we also get in *her* head?" I ask. "What if it gives us a way to prove this baby isn't yours?"

"Why are you so sure it isn't?"

I press my lips together. "Intuition mixed with total distrust."

I hear some loud voices in the background. "I hate to get off the phone in the middle of this conversation, but I have one more meeting I need to get to. Do you want me to try calling her again?"

"No," I say. "Let's let her move in. Let's play her game."

"Are you sure?" he asks. I'm sure he wants to say more but he can't since he has to get to his meeting. It's fine. I can handle it.

"Nope. Not at all. But it gives me a week alone with her before you get back, and if she drives me bananas, I'll stay with Nicki."

"Just be careful," he says. "I think this is a bad idea. I don't want her to hurt you. And I don't want anything that happens between the two of you to jeopardize my career."

"It won't," I say, my voice adamant. "I've got this. And thank you again for what you did for me. You can tell me you're not a Prince Charming until the end of time, but I'll keep right on believing you are."

"And I'll keep finding ways to prove I'm not."

We'll see about that.

CHAPTER 17

"Ellie, no. What the hell are you doing?" Nicki asks me.

We're hanging out at Luke's house—*our* house—eating ice cream and I just nonchalantly confessed that Michelle is moving in on Friday.

I shrug. "I don't really know, to be perfectly honest. But it has to be better knowing the devil you're dealing with than waiting for more bombs to drop, right?"

She shakes her head and makes a face. "No! This is a terrible idea."

"I know it's a terrible idea," I admit, "but it's also currently the only idea that I have to protect Luke. That's what this is all about. Starting the moment he hired me as his publicist, and going through our wedding up to now, my goal has remained the same. Protect Luke, whether it's protecting his job, his personal life, or himself, that's my whole purpose here."

"How is living with the woman your husband knocked up and hurting yourself in the process protecting him in any way whatsoever?" she asks.

"It's making him look good to his boss," I point out.

"So does sending a thank you card."

My brows dip. "Was he supposed to send a thank you card?"

She blows out an exasperated breath. "We just sent one for his wedding gift."

"Oh. We didn't get one of those from him," I say. "See? He already hates us."

"Because you didn't tell anyone about the wedding. Remember?"

"Yeah, yeah. And I get what you're saying. There are other, easier ways to look good to the boss. But this is a delicate situation, Nicki. Luke is so afraid of Michelle and her father that he *married* me. He won't stand up to her...but I will."

"Won't that be even worse?"

I lift a shoulder. "You know me. I'll just be sweet and charming."

Nicki snort-laughs. Yeah, I might have my work cut out for me when it comes to Michelle.

"So why, exactly, is this how you're choosing to handle it?" she asks.

"Because this gives me the inside track. It lets me be as close to her as I can be. Keep your enemies close, right?" I ask. "Can't get much closer than living together."

"I guess. But won't you feel like a prisoner in your own home? You can't say anything in front of her. You'll have to pretend all the time. And what if she's listening? What if she plants devices or video records you?"

"All things I've thought of. Luke has a surveillance system already in place, so if she plants anything or even tries anything, we'll know about it. We'll keycode our bedroom door and offices. She'll only have access to the places in the house we want her to. And what if *I* am the one listening? What if I hear her admit that it's not Luke's?"

Nicki rolls her eyes. "Are you really on that train again? This is Michelle. She's slightly delusional, yes, but this isn't some soap opera, Elle. This is real life, and she's not going to *lie* about who the father is."

I press my lips together. "You really don't think so? In your version of *real life*, do families oust one member as the black sheep? Do parents choose their favorite child and make it really obvious when they do? Do sisters betray their brother's confidence on their freaking wedding day? Do brothers sleep with the same woman?"

"I take it you're talking about the Daltons."

I give her a *duh* look and shove a big spoonful of cookie dough ice cream in my mouth.

"I mean, obviously you're looking for a yes, but I just don't think Michelle would do that. Not with her dad's vested interest in Luke."

"That may be true. But don't you think desperate people have done far worse than lying about a baby's true paternity?" I ask.

"Maybe," she concedes.

"I'll get to the bottom of it," I say resolutely.

She points her spoon at me. "Just be careful."

* * *

In a twist of fate that I never would have believed, a moving truck actually shows up at the house on Friday.

And in another twist I still can't believe, I don't send it away. In fact, I welcome Michelle into our home. Not quite with arms wide open, but something along those lines.

The truck arrives before she does, and the movers ask me where to put her stuff. I guide them toward the bedroom off the second family room. It's the furthest away from our bedroom and gives us the most space from her while living in the same house.

My heart races when she walks in the door with the movers on their third or fourth trip in. I didn't expect her to ring the bell, and certainly not when she feels so entitled to be here that she is moving in uninvited, yet I don't like how it feels. I don't like her walking in without me knowing that she's here, but since my big idea is to just let it happen, it's something I guess I'm just going to have to get used to.

"Happy move in day," I say with far more enthusiasm than I feel.

She purses her lips rather than giving me a friendly response. "Where, exactly, are you putting me?"

"I figured you'd appreciate having some privacy, so your bedroom is the one off the second family room. Nice view of the backyard and plenty of space just for you." I smile sweetly.

"So you're basically separating me from the rest of the house? Putting me next to the dog's room?" She's whining already. Good Lord, this is not what I signed up for.

Except...it is. And I'm still not really sure why.

"The placement of your room is for you as much as it is for us. We're here to help you through this pregnancy, but ultimately we all have our own lives to live. I'm sure you don't want the room right next to the master bedroom so you can listen to everything newlyweds do in their spare time."

"Oh, honey," she says condescendingly. "Your husband won't have any spare time."

I raise a brow. "Excuse me?"

"I've scheduled my appointments for the baby on Tuesdays. And I do expect they'll take all day. I sure hope you've found something to occupy your time since your *husband* will be busy taking care of me." She gives me a smile like she thinks she's won.

Oh, quite the contrary.

"Actually, I do have something to occupy my time. My *husband* recently gave me all the tools to start my own business since he believes so strongly in my abilities. So I'll be quite busy as I launch my new company. I do hope you have something to occupy your time as well since as much as I'd love to sit around and chat all day, I simply won't have the time." I smile sweetly back at her.

When she came up with this demented plan to move in here, she probably thought I'd just lie down for her. Since Luke is incapable of standing up to her because he feels shoved between a rock and a hard place, I'd be willing to bet that with a father as powerful as hers, she's spent her entire life walking over people who fear what she has the ability to do.

But I'm not scared of her. And that's what prompts the next words to fall out of my mouth. I know he won't say it, and I'm here to protect him...to protect both of us. "Oh, and by the way, before you trap my husband further into your web, I'm going to need a paternity test to prove that he's really the father of that child you're carrying."

Her eyes widen and an ugly snarl twists her face. "How could you even insinuate that this child isn't Luke's?"

I take a step closer to her. I'm maybe the least intimidating person in the world, but I refuse to be trampled by this bitch. "Because I don't trust you. Until I have definitive proof that it's his, I'm not participating in the games you're playing." And it's not just that. If I hadn't gone to the doctor's appointment and saw the baby with my own eyes on that screen, I'm not entirely sure I'd even believe she's pregnant.

She laughs like the thought is simply absurd. "Sure you're not. If that were true, would I really be moving in today?"

I give her another sweet smile. "Really gives you something to think about, doesn't it? I have to get to work now, but good luck with the unpacking. Take it slow and don't lift anything too heavy." And with those as my parting words, I stalk out of the room toward my office, slip in my earbuds to drown her out, and get to work.

CHAPTER 18

Five more days.

In five days, Luke will be back home, and I'm praying I don't kill her before then. It's not looking good.

I'm being a little dramatic, but I can't stand living with Michelle. I can't exactly confess that to Luke since I approved this from the start, but she's a terrible roommate. She doesn't just leave wet coffee spoons in the sugar bowl, though she does do that after jumping on the defensive to say she's just having one cup of decaf since too much caffeine is bad for the baby.

She apparently knows everything about everything because she reads blog posts about mom life, she's the first person ever to get nauseous during pregnancy, and she's more worried about whether her child will be attractive than smart.

She also listens to awful music way too loudly—so loudly, in fact, that even Pepper runs outside just to get away from it. It's a huge house, yet I can still hear the beat of the bass in my office. Is that good for the baby?

I'm trying to be supportive here, but I'm realizing far too late that I should've put up a much, much bigger fight about her moving in. Nicki was right.

At least I can still drink, unlike poor Michelle who's apparently also the first person who ever had to give up alcohol during pregnancy and it's just the worst thing in the world—except for her aching feet.

I roll my eyes about four hundred thousand times a day, and I leave the house to work at Starbucks just to get away from her.

Four more days.

In four days, Luke will be back home, and I've had to sit on my hands so I don't strangle her. But Luke arranged for me to go with her to her next doctor's visit today, and I'm going in with a question.

"You don't have to come into the actual exam room with me," she says when her name is called by the nurse.

"Oh, that's okay. I'd love to come." I give her the sweet smile that I've started referring to in my own mind as my *Michelle smile.*

The doctor walks in and eyes me.

"This is Ellie," Michelle says.

"Hi. The wife of the father." I give a little wave.

The doctor's brows dip a little, but she doesn't say anything. I imagine she's seen far worse in this room. "I'm Dr. Pruitt," she says, and she moves to examine Michelle. I turn away to give her privacy.

"Any questions?" the doctor asks at the end of the exam. She glances at me as if to ask if I have questions, too.

"Yes, I have one," I say. "How invasive is a paternity test?"

"Totally non-invasive and safe for both the baby and the mother with a simple blood draw. We'll need the father's blood, too, for comparison. Are you interested?" Dr. Pruitt asks.

"Yes," I say at the same time Michelle says, "No." Both of us are firm.

"It's just...we're not *totally* sure that my husband is the father seeing as how he doesn't even remember the night Michelle says she got pregnant." I wrinkle my nose and say it under my breath like I'm revealing a little hush-hush secret.

Dr. Pruitt nods with understanding. "I see. Michelle, you have to get a blood draw today anyway. If you're interested, they can grab an extra vial for paternity testing while you're back there."

"I, uh…" Michelle says, sputtering a little. "I'm just terrified of needles. I'd rather not."

"You'll be fine," I say, my voice flat. "They have to draw anyway, so let's just get it done, okay?"

The doctor looks back and forth between us. "It's not my place to get involved, but I also can't watch someone coerce my patient into something she doesn't want to do," she says to me.

"I'm sorry," I lie. "Michelle, do you have some reason why you're not okay with getting this test done? I'm sure Luke would love to know."

Michelle sighs. "No, it's fine. Let's just get it over with."

The doctor nods. "You can go back to the lab for your bloodwork. I'll put in the paperwork for an extra vial."

"Thank you, Dr. Pruitt," Michelle says softly.

The doctor glances at me again before looking back at Michelle. "Would you like to talk privately, Ms. Bennett?"

"No, it's fine," she says softly, her tone full of reluctance.

"Would you excuse us?" Dr. Pruitt says to me.

I hold up both hands. "Of course," I say, and I exit the room.

They talk for a few brief moments, and then the doctor exits. She brushes past me without another glance.

Michelle emerges a minute later and we walk back to the lab together. She draws in a few deep breaths. She really is scared to get this bloodwork done.

"It's okay," I say to her. "No big deal. Just don't look at the needle and you'll be fine."

She glares at me. Whatever. I was just trying to be helpful.

Her name is called, and she's all shaky when she walks up to get her blood taken. I watch through the window as they put the elastic band on her arm and tap around for a vein. She closes her eyes and turns away when they insert the needle.

"Stop!" she yells after a few seconds. "Stop. I'm going to pass ou..." the end of her sentence trails off as she actually does pass out.

My heart races as I watch the phlebotomists rush around as they get her cold water, removing the needle from her arm and bandaging it up. They reposition her with her head between her legs as she comes to, and my heart rate starts to even out when I see that she's fine.

They only got one vial—the routine one they needed for her test, not the extra one we requested.

There goes another chance to find out whether Luke is really the father, and with the chance goes my hopes right down the drain.

And it's not just that.

I feel like shit for making her pass out.

I drive her car back home, and I make her dinner, and by *make her dinner*, I mean I reheat something Debbie left for us. By the time she's done eating and leaves her plate on the kitchen table like I'm her maid, well, I'm done feeling bad.

And when Luke calls, I'm even more done if that's such a thing.

"You made Michelle pass out?" he asks.

"Is that what she told you?" I feel like he's immediately putting me on the defensive. He didn't ask about me or my day. He asked about *her*.

"Basically."

"And you believed her?" I ask.

"Well? What happened?"

"She had to get her blood drawn. The doctor called in an extra vial of blood for the paternity test, and she passed out on vial one. We didn't get it."

"Babe, you can't push her into stuff she doesn't want to do," he says gently.

"I didn't," I say thickly. "She agreed to it."

"Yeah, under duress. She's pregnant. You have to be more careful with her."

"I'm fully aware that she's pregnant," I spit. "I'm the one currently living with her."

"By your own choice. I told you it was a terrible idea," he says.

"Nice time to throw that in my face. And way to let her come between us. A-freaking-gain." I hang up. It's childish, but I'm pissed.

I hate leaving things that way with Luke, but it is what it is. The distance is clearly getting to us. So is Michelle.

But even though I'm mad at him, I know this is worth hanging onto—at the very least, hanging onto it to make it bearable for the next year. But also for so much more than that...I hope.

Three more days.

Michelle has some friends over. They cackle loudly about how she gets to live here even though Luke is married to someone else now.

I roll my eyes at Debbie, who chuckles, but later she reminds me how she's never seen Luke as happy as he is with me.

Two more days.

Michelle leaves a mess on the stove after making eggs and burns toast so badly she actually set off the smoke detector.

Tomorrow Luke will be home.

Oddly, Michelle spends most of her day at the office. I guess as the Aces get closer to coming back home, work for her starts to get a little busier. Lest anyone's overly concerned, though, Michelle's father cut her hours in half so she has time to rest. Her paycheck is apparently the same, though, not that it's any of my business. Lucky her for being born into a rich family.

And then, after two long weeks apart, the laundry room door opens. "Honey, I'm home," a charming, deep, and very familiar voice calls out.

I scramble from my place on the couch to get to him first, but I'm not fast enough. Pepper runs toward him, and then there's our new roommate.

"Thank God you're here," Michelle says, rushing past me. "Ellie has just been so mean to me!"

Oh. My. God.

I clench my fists so tightly my nails dig into my palms as I watch her toss her arms around his neck, practically kicking Pepper on her way by. Pepper whimpers a little.

"Excuse me," Luke says, untangling himself from her. He gently moves her aside, reaches down to scratch Pepper on the head, then walks past Michelle and over to me. He pulls me into his arms and a certain heat passes between us for a beat. His eyes crinkle as a smile lights his whole face.

And then his mouth crashes down to mine as my arms link around him, and he kisses me—really kisses me good and hard—for a full minute before he pulls away and we come up for air.

"God, I missed you," he says, punctuating his words with smaller kisses to my mouth.

"I missed you, too," I say, my chest tight as I kiss him back. I feel it with every fiber of my being.

This isn't for show. This isn't part of an act. This is two people who spent nearly every waking minute together and then were forced apart for two of the longest weeks of either of their lives. This is two people who desperately missed each other as one held a piece of the other's heart across the miles.

We're both whole again now that we're back together, and neither of us cares that someone is watching. This isn't about her. It's about a husband and his wife and the love that has blossomed between us.

"Get your sweet little ass upstairs," he says softly.

I know she heard, but I don't care. I don't care what her reaction is. Instead, I don't even look at her as I follow his directions.

"I'll be right up," he says after my retreating figure.

Every part of me wants to stay and listen to what he has to say to Michelle, but I give them their moment together. He pushed past her for me, and a feeling of joy rushes through my chest.

He isn't going to let her come between us.

CHAPTER 19

I sit waiting as patiently as humanly possible on the bed. Should I get naked? Or do I let him do it? Is he even coming up here for sex? God, I hope so.

I'm desperate to be with him again. It's only been two weeks, but those two weeks were filled with emotional ups and downs. I don't think I realized how attached I'd become to him until he was gone. And it's not just that physical attachment. I feel it deep in my chest, down into my soul.

I need this time with him. I need to feel him as he pushes into me, to strengthen our bodily connection again as we continue to nurture our emotional one.

I'm giddy as I wait. I bounce up and down a little, and I shake my hands out to try to burn some of my nervous energy. The door opens. My heart races.

He kicks it shut behind him, and he locks it for good measure. He's clutching his duffel bag, which he drops to the floor as his eyes meet mine. And then he stalks slowly across the room toward me, his eyes hot on mine the entire time.

He kicks off his shoes as he walks, and he doesn't waste a single second. He pulls his shirt over his head, tossing it to the floor as my eyes fall to his abs. Those sweet, sweet abs I missed so damn much.

He moves between my legs, gently pushes me back, and climbs on the bed until he hovers over me. Our eyes lock for one hot beat before he lowers his mouth to mine.

His mouth opens to mine and our tongues brush as all the aching need I've felt since the moment he walked out the door intensifies to unbearable levels. I push my hips toward his as I seek some sort of relief, but it'll take more than a little humping to alleviate my burning need.

My nails glide up his back, and he grunts into me as our tongues continue to batter each other's. He deepens the kiss, somehow making it more intense and more intimate as he lowers himself down, his heat warming me all over. And then, out of nowhere, he flips us so I'm on top of him, straddling his hips. He doesn't break our kiss when he moves us, but I do. I sit up on his lap and grind my hips over his. I feel how hard he is for me. I feel how *ready* he is for me, and I'm just as ready.

He groans as I continue shifting my hips over him, and then I reach for the hem of my shirt and rip it over my head. I toss it to the floor and then I unhook my bra, throwing it across the room. He runs his palms along my torso, stopping to cup my breasts. His hands are rougher than they were the last time he touched me, but just the feel of his touch on my bare skin sends me into another stratosphere.

I close my eyes and moan as I lean my head back, jutting my breasts forward automatically to give him a better angle to work with. His thumb brushes my nipples, and I whimper as the feeling sends an arrow of need through my entire core.

He does it again and again, and the whimper turns into a moan.

He shifts us again, setting me to the side of him but only long enough to get rid of his sweatpants. I get rid of my jeans and my panties while we're at it, and I don't think a single word has been spoken since he walked into this room. Our bodies are doing all the talking for us. There will be plenty of time to catch up later. Plenty of time to argue and fight. Plenty of time to make up and talk.

Right now, though, we both need this.

He urges me over toward him so I'm straddling him. I'm about to reach down and fist his cock when I notice the bruises all over his arms and chest. I run a finger softly along one of them on his biceps, and he winces a bit. No wonder why he wants me on top. The poor guy is hurting, but that's not going to stop him—or me—from the release we're both desperate for.

Finally, I reach down, grab his shaft in my fist, and pump up and down a few times. His eyes close as his face twists with pleasure, and then I line him up and lower myself onto his waiting cock.

We both groan at the perfection of his body entering mine. I move over him so he slides almost all the way out before I shove my hips back down so he's as far in as our bodies physically will let him be.

I cry out as he fills me, and then I move up again before slamming back down. "Oh fuck, Ellie," he murmurs, and his curse only goads me on to pick up my pace. Up and down, in and out, up and down, in and out. We find a rhythm together as he holds me under my ass, helping direct our speed. One of his fingers inches over to the tight bud in back, and I stiffen as he presses into a place that I'd still categorize as virgin territory.

I'm already filled in front, and this new and foreign sensation seems to fill me even more. The heat between us mixes with this prohibited, illicit feeling, and it's mere seconds before my body convulses into a climax.

I scream out as pleasure rips through me, and his finger continues to push into the forbidden area as I come and come. The contractions of my body send him into his own release. He growls as his hips jerk up to meet mine, and then he grunts a string of curses that are absolute music to my ears as I listen to him ride the wave of bliss.

It's over far too soon.

I know we'll do that again. I know there's more in store for us. But every time we're in the midst of our passion, I want it to last forever. Despite how good it feels to come, I can't help but feel a little sad when it's over and we're forced to break our sweet connection.

We do, though. I shift up so he slides out of me, and I lie beside him for a few quiet minutes, both of us panting as we try to regain our breath.

"Well that was fun," he says after a few quiet beats pass between us.

I giggle and turn on my side to face him, and I find him already on his side facing me. I run a fingertip over his eyebrow. "I missed you," I say.

His lips tip up. "I missed you, too. No more letting her come between us, okay? And for the love of all things holy, don't fucking hang up on me."

"I'm sorry," I say, heat creeping into my cheeks. He's right. It was childish.

"It's okay. I love you, Ellie."

"I love you, too."

I just hope that love is enough for us to overcome all the obstacles that lie ahead of us.

CHAPTER 20

"Seriously, be a little louder next time," Michelle mutters sarcastically as we walk into the kitchen hand-in-hand after our nice little welcome home romp.

"You're the one who wanted to move in with the newlyweds," I shoot back.

Luke gives me a look of warning, and if we were on the phone, I'd be tempted to hang up on him.

"But we'll try to keep it down," I amend, and Luke gives me a look of gratitude for attempting to keep the peace. This can't be easy on him. She's already ruining the sugar bowl again, and just when he thought he was rid of her, she's back.

Letting her move in was a stupid, stupid mistake, but it takes exactly one more little bitch fest between the two of us for me to realize how very, very stuck we are.

"Stop putting your wet coffee spoon in the sugar bowl," I snarl at Michelle after dinner.

She looks at me in surprise. "I had no idea it bothered you so much. You don't even use the sugar."

"Because it's all hard and crusty from your wet spoon." *You fucking slob.* I don't say that last part aloud, obviously.

"Ladies," Luke booms. We both look at him in surprise where he still sits at the kitchen table. Even Pepper pauses in chewing on her dog bone to glance up at him. "Just stop. Don't pick fights with each other. I just need some peace and quiet at home, and if I can't get it here, I'll go stay with Josh during training camp. Is that what you want?"

"No," Michelle says at the same time I say, "I'm sorry."

"Just knock it off," he says, and he stalks out of the room.

"This is your fault," she says to me as soon as he's gone.

I sigh. "How, exactly, is it my fault?"

"Just shut up about the goddamn coffee spoon." She glares at me like I'm an idiot. "Luke doesn't care about shit like that."

"God, Michelle. You don't know one damn thing about him."

Her brows dip like she doesn't quite get it, and I realize then it's because she *doesn't get it*. The first night we met, he confessed the coffee spoon in the sugar bowl thing. Before we knew a damn thing about each other, that was the first thing he said. He was joking that it was the reason they broke up, but clearly it was those little things that got to him first, and it was the big things that caused the eventual split.

And now he's literally stuck with her for the rest of his life because they share a child.

The only way out of this is finding out it's not his baby...but the odds aren't looking good on that front.

I stalk out of the room and head upstairs. "Can we talk?" I ask when I find Luke collapsed on the chair in our bedroom as he looks out over the backyard.

"Sure," he says. He makes no attempt to move.

"I'm sorry I let her move in."

He sighs. "It's not your fault. It's mine. I should've been clear with her from the start of that conversation."

"Why weren't you?" I ask gently.

"I had a lot on my mind. Camp isn't just about practice and game strategy. It's about fighting like hell for your position. I hate competing against Josh, but it felt like it was the two of us against each other, against the second-string guys, against the new guys."

"Who won the battle?" I ask, genuinely curious about the answer.

He shakes his head. "Nobody yet. We still have nearly two full weeks of camp here at home before we really have a clear answer. Last year Josh and I were the top two. But this kid right out of college is fast as fuck and he's posing a real threat."

"I get it. It's a lot to worry about, and you don't need Michelle and me fighting here when you need to focus on the game."

"No, I don't," he says. "You're right. But you're both here, and we have to learn to live with that. As much as she drives me up the fucking wall, as much as I don't want her here and don't want to live with her, the reality is that she's carrying my child. It's too early for her to be here, but I'd sort of thought I'd ask her to move in when the baby gets here anyway. So I guess we're just a few months ahead of schedule."

"There are ways for you to see the baby without the two of you living together," I say. *If the baby's even yours.*

"I don't want to just *see the baby*. I want to be an active part of its life. I already have a fucked up schedule because of my job, so this is the only way I'll get full access to my own child."

"Unless you sue for full custody," I point out.

"Which I can't do." He gives me a look like I'm insane.

"Why not? You have rights, Luke."

"I realize that," he says with frustration. "But so does she. I can't just take the baby away from its mother. Besides, what would Calvin think?"

For as much as he doesn't give a shit what his own family thinks, he's sure hung up on what Calvin might think. I get it since Calvin holds Luke's career in his hands, but that doesn't make it any less frustrating.

I sigh but I don't really have a response to that.

"I can't exactly kick her out now," he finally says. "Just stay away from her. Do your own thing. Don't let her get to you. We just have to deal with her."

"Okay," I say, trying to keep my own frustration out of my tone. I'm not sure I succeed.

But I *will* succeed in being the bigger person. I won't let Michelle come between Luke and me.

CHAPTER 21

I've been to plenty of football games over the course of my brother's career, but my focus was always on nachos and beer, not on actually watching the game. I went for the social connection, for the fun of being there and people watching while I sat with family or friends sometimes in the stands and sometimes in a suite.

Today we're in a suite, and this just *feels* different than all those other games.

Today I'm going in to actually watch the game, to see my *husband* as he takes the field with his teammates after a couple weeks away for training camp, to hold my breath with every snap of the ball as I pray for an injury-free game.

I guess it doesn't just feel different. It *is* different.

I'm too nervous to eat. *It's just a preseason game.* I remember Josh saying that back in Chicago, like they don't *really* matter compared to regular season games.

But the risk is still there. Every time Luke steps out onto the field, he's putting his body at risk. His safety. His health.

I never cared when it was my brother doing it, but it's a completely different realm when it's the man you love going out there.

We were out the door by ten-thirty after we ate Lucky Charms and blueberry waffles with peanut butter spread on top. We drove to the stadium with Nicki and Josh, and I saw the way she wrung her hands in her lap as my brother drove. I saw the way Luke locked up and got real quiet the closer we got to the stadium. I saw the way my brother focused on traffic. Everyone in the car was silent as we approached the stadium, and Luke gave me a kiss before he headed to the locker room with my brother.

"Go get 'em," I said to him, and he smiled at me, pressed one more kiss to my lips, and turned away. "And be safe, Luke," I called after him. He turned back and winked at me, and it felt like the start of a new tradition, like I will say those words to him hundreds of times.

We watch from our suite as the stands begin to fill. I can't help but wonder what Luke is doing right now. Probably listening to his pregame playlist, and I still haven't gotten out of him which playlist it is or what's on it. He seems private about it, so I will continue to believe it's a power mix of ballads from Celine Dion, Adele, and Whitney Houston until he proves otherwise.

Leah, Krista, and Nadine are in our suite, too, along with Mo and a couple other women who Nicki just introduced me to.

"Does it always feel like this?" I ask Nicki when we're seated by ourselves in the second row of our suite as the others mill around the buffet table behind us.

"Like what?" she asks, glancing over at me.

"Like you're freaking out a little on the inside that he's going to get hurt and you want him so badly to pull out a win and be the big savior of the game and it feels like it's a personal attack against you if all that doesn't happen."

She grunts a small chuckle. "Yeah. Except you'll freak out a *lot* on the inside, not a little. Especially when it comes to the regular season. I'd be surprised if they put Luke and Josh in for more than a quarter today. They have to keep their best players healthy." She keeps her eyes focused on the field. "The worst thing in the world would be for either of them to get hurt during a game that doesn't even matter."

"Yeah," I say absently.

"And whatever you do, don't talk about contracts or give away any inside vulnerable information to the other wives." She says it softly, but it's a clear warning. "You can't put yourself in a vulnerable position, either."

I look at her with brows drawn in together. "Why not?"

She shakes her head. "We'll talk more about it later, but just know that every single time your husband gets out on that field, he's fighting for his spot to play there. And he might be fighting against the husband of the woman sitting behind you. He might be fighting against your best friend's husband. You can be real with me, obviously, but there's a set of unwritten rules we need to follow."

I nod, and it's just then that the women settle into their seats with plates of food in front of us and behind us and Mo slides into the seat beside me.

"How's the first game so far as a football wife?" she asks.

I tuck away Nicki's hushed warnings for now, but I keep them close. "Considering we haven't even started yet, so far, so good."

She chuckles. "You feeling the nerves already?"

I glance at her plate of food. "I can't even eat."

"It does take some getting used to. It's easier now that Mitch is a coach and not player anymore. I don't have to worry about *him* getting injured, but I do have every other man out on that field to worry about. They're all my boys—including your Luke."

I smile. She's really like the team mother, and she's helping me feel more at ease.

"I heard Michelle Bennett moved in with you. Is that true?" she asks, her voice low so this conversation is just between us.

That doesn't make it any more comfortable, though. This just seems like the wrong place to gossip about the owner's daughter.

"Yeah, it's true," I admit. I glance around to be sure nobody's listening. "And I hate her." I cover my mouth with my hand.

Oh shit. After Nicki's warning literally five seconds ago, I'm already showing a vulnerability that I probably shouldn't—especially not to the coach's wife, even if she's here for us and heads up the wives' club.

Mo laughs, but she doesn't just laugh. It's a good, solid belly laugh, and she's wiping her eyes by the time she's done. In fact, she's laughing so loudly and so heartily that she draws the attention of some of the women in our suite. They pause their conversations to glance over to see what's so funny.

I guess letting that little vulnerability slip out wasn't my worst mistake.

"I'm sorry," she says as she tries to catch her breath. She leans in close as she calms down and the others return to their own conversations. "You're far from the first person to tell me that. I'll keep my own opinions to myself, but for what it's worth, Mitch has come home raving about Luke's newfound fire. We both attribute that to you. So keep pushing. Keep walking beside him. Keep holding his hand. He didn't have that fire when he was with her. He'll be down on that field playing for *you* today, not for her. Never for her."

It's my turn to wipe my eyes, but not because I'm laughing. I hold her words close to my heart.

A few minutes later, the announcer calls the opposing team to the field. They run out to their sideline, and then the announcer says, "And now, your Vegas Aces!"

The crowd filling the stands goes wild, deafening screams all around for the hometown heroes as they run onto the field.

I find the *DALTON* eighty-four jersey right away as he runs beside *NOLAN* number eighteen, the same number my brother has worn since he was in peewee league. My heart races, and I can't imagine what he's feeling down on that field if I'm feeling it so strongly up here watching him. Is this just something he's used to dealing with? Or does he get nervous before each game?

Is he as worried about getting hurt as I am?

The game starts, and I find myself on the edge of my seat as I start to wonder why I didn't pick up a love for this sport ages ago. I guess I'm a little more invested now that the guy I married is on the field. And Nicki's right. Both Luke and Josh only play the first quarter. They're on the sidelines with baseball caps instead of helmets and towels slung around their necks as they watch their teammates give a real beating to the Seahawks.

I'm relieved when the game is over even though Luke spends most of the time on the sidelines. I do manage to get myself some nachos at the half, but only because he isn't playing.

Nicki leads me down to the post-game room, where wives, girlfriends, kids, and families wait for their players to emerge from the locker room. The first one comes out about a half hour after the end of the game. Nicki explains how the coach says a few words, they head off to showers, and then they have interviews with the media, so we'll usually have to wait about an hour. And she's right on the money. Luke walks out with Josh, both of them looking exhausted as they walk slowly toward us.

Nicki beelines for my brother, and I watch as she inspects a shiny bruise on his arm after kissing him.

Luke pulls me into his arms and leans his forehead down to mine.

"Good game," I say softly.

"Thanks," he murmurs. He draws in a deep breath.

"Hey, you okay?" I back up a little so I can get a look at him.

He leans down to kiss me softly. "Better now," he says.

I melt, and then I mirror my best friend as I inspect his arms for new bruises. I see a few scratches, too. "How'd these happen?" I ask, lightly fingering near them.

"The turf is rougher than it looks. Especially when a lineman slams you to the ground and you slide across it."

I wince.

"It's fine," he says, clearly trying to be the tough guy and especially here, where ears of teammates who want his position might be listening. I never realized how protective he needs to be over his place on the team until Nicki pointed it out just before today's game started.

I glance around at the men gathered. They're all moving just a little more slowly than they were when they pranced in this morning, but it's because they all just took a beating out on that field even though they won. I can't help but wonder why they do this to themselves.

And even though we're not supposed to talk about it, I can't help but wonder what comes next.

CHAPTER 22

The next preseason game is an away game, and I've hardly seen Luke all week since he's been at camp all day every day. He comes home bruised and exhausted, and our conversations are short as he goes to bed nearly immediately after he walks in the door and he's out the door before sunrise.

It's an intense, hard schedule, but it's one he has to keep up in order to keep his place on the Aces. I guess I'm starting to get it now.

He loves this game. It's his life. It's his path and his passion.

But he's in a contract year. He's one bad landing, one hit too hard, one injury away from early retirement. He's one conversation with the boss that goes the wrong way from being traded. He has proven his worth over the last nine years, but no matter how indispensable I make him to the team, ultimately if he doesn't perform on the field, it doesn't matter.

Fans can love him, and we can post his thirst traps, but those things won't keep him here.

He can still contribute to the community wherever he lands. It'll make him attractive to other teams, I suppose. But he doesn't want to go to another team, something he's made very clear.

I keep to my side of the house and avoid Michelle at all costs.

They lose the second preseason game, which I don't attend since it's in New Orleans. Of course we can travel to any game we wish, just as anybody can, but Nicki explained that traditionally wives stay home for the preseason away games. Many of the wives have children, and some have their own jobs, but all have responsibilities back home that make it difficult to take off for three days. Traveling is part of the deal for Luke and the other guys. Their hotel rooms and meals are included, and it's not like I'd be taking a vacation with my husband since it's not really part of the deal for spouses.

But Nicki and I have made plans to go to the first game of the season in a few weeks.

Luke informs me that he played exactly four plays anyway—not because he wasn't needed, but because they benched their top players early to keep them healthy when the other team had scored twice in the first few possessions.

There are two more preseason games, and this coming weekend is at home against the Broncos.

That means Jack will be in town.

I'm hopeful we don't have to see him, but I haven't gotten the official word yet from Luke as he goes into his final week of training camp.

He's practicing at the stadium on Friday when the doorbell rings mid-morning. I'm in my office, and I have no idea where Michelle is—nor do I care—as I stand and head down the hallway toward the foyer.

But apparently Michelle *is* home because she beats me there. I hear voices as I approach that direction, and I quiet my steps. I stop, standing just around the corner from them to listen.

"Is she home?" the voice is low, but not too low to miss his words. I immediately recognize it.

"Yeah," Michelle says softly. I hear the telltale smack of a quick, stolen kiss.

Wait a minute.

Michelle and Jack are *kissing* now?

"You shouldn't be here."

"I know," he says. "I figured it would be easy to play it off that I was visiting my brother."

She laughs. "He's not even home. He's at practice."

What the hell?

And...what the fuck?

How do I even play this little twist?

"Come on in," she says a little louder, and I choose that moment to walk into the hallway.

They look up at me in surprise, and I don't have to fake the surprise on my own face. "Jack. What are you doing here?"

"Oh, just came to see my brother, but Michelle tells me he isn't home," he says. He's just as handsome as I remember, somehow so devilishly charming with just a single glance in my direction, but I won't fall for it.

"Well he's not here, so you can feel free to slither back to wherever you came from." I smile sweetly, giving him the *Michelle smile* I've come to perfect over the last few weeks.

"Oh, but I have a whole two hours free, so I'd love to get to know my new sister-in-law a little better," he says.

I give him a tight smile. "Some of us have jobs," I say, glancing over at Michelle pointedly as I wonder why she isn't at hers, "so I'm unable to entertain you at the moment."

"I can entertain you," Michelle says. "I'm free all day."

I wonder exactly what sort of entertaining Michelle is going to be doing, but I really do have work to do. Greg sent me the contact information for three of the Aces teammates who are interested in my services, so I have three plans to draft to try to sell them on why they need PCPR to handle their publicity. Each of the three has slightly different goals, so it's not just some easy cut and paste job. I need to be precise as I tailor plans to each man.

"It's as lovely as ever to see you, Jack," I say with as much sincerity as I can muster. It's true. It's as lovely as ever—which isn't very lovely at all. "I hope you lose on Sunday." I smirk and turn to leave as he bellows out a laugh.

"Oh, silly, sweet, misguided Ellie." His tone is mocking, and I want to slap him. "You really don't know much about the game, do you?" I turn back around at his insult to find him leering in my direction. "Not only are we going to beat the Aces, but we're going to beat them handily. Tell Luke to watch out for Allen Hammond." He winks at me, and I repeat the name three times to myself so I can look him up when I get back to my office.

"Break a leg," I say back, meaning those words literally rather than figuratively. "Oh, sorry. Is that appropriate for football? Or is that more suited for drama?" I shrug and play dumb. "Well, plenty of drama here, am I right?" I leave those as my parting words as I head back toward my office.

The first thing I do is type *Allen Hammond* into the search bar. I learn he's a safety for the Broncos. I look up what a safety does and discover that their job is to stop the offense from scoring at all costs.

And then I look up a little more on Allen. Apparently he's known for his extremely aggressive behavior when it comes to stopping wide receivers. He's famous for launching himself into opponents trying to catch the ball, in particular shoving a shoulder into their chests to knock the wind out of them and hurt them just enough to sideline them for a few plays. He's intentional with his hits, but he doesn't catch penalties since there's nothing illegal about chest hits.

I'm sure Luke knows how to deal with aggressive safeties. It's part of his job, after all.

But this just gives me one more thing to worry about.

CHAPTER 23

The three of us sit down to dinner an hour after Luke gets home. Today's training camp session was slightly less intense than previous days to give players a bit of a break to rest before Sunday's game. Luke's plate is nearly empty, and I'm almost done, too. Michelle takes an hour and a half to eat three bites of pasta, and I don't have the energy to play hostess to her tonight.

Especially not when I need answers.

My plate is empty, and I take mine and Luke's to the sink when I decide I can't sit on this any longer. Rather than talk privately to Luke, rather than stew over it, rather than have a conversation with Michelle, I blurt out the question that's weighed on my mind since this afternoon when I return to the table.

"Hey, Michelle, you want to explain to Luke and me why you and Jack kissed earlier?"

Her eyes widen as she looks across the table at me.

She's caught, and her expression says it all. Not only did I catch her doing something she didn't think I knew about, but I also caught her off guard with my question.

Her eyes edge over to Luke to gauge his reaction.

"It was a friendly greeting," she says, brushing off my accusatory tone. "He's become a good friend to me the last few weeks."

I nod, my expression dripping with sarcasm. "Right. So that's why you told him he shouldn't be here and he said something about it being easy to pretend he's here to visit Luke."

Her brows dip. She had no idea that I heard everything.

"He said *what?*" Luke asks. "He wouldn't come here to see me. Not before a game." He turns his angry gaze on Michelle. "What was he doing here?"

"I told you, he's become a good friend to me," she says. She's maintaining her cool, but there are little things that tip me off to the truth. The way her eyes dart around a little like she's trying to come up with a sufficient lie, for example. The way she taps her fork lightly against her plate without even realizing she's doing it. The way she takes a big bite of pasta to fill her mouth so she can think up more lies.

"How *good?*" Luke sneers, his tone full of innuendo.

"Why do you even care? It's not like you want to be with me."

Luke lets out a maniacal little laugh. "No, you're certainly right about that. But I have a right to know. You're carrying my child and you're living in my house while claiming you're still in love with me. Are you sleeping with my brother?"

She smirks. "Wouldn't that be great if I was? A great way to poke the beast in you. To get you to wake up and see you should be with me."

I roll my eyes. I can't even muster up a good response to that joke of a line.

"You still haven't answered my question," Luke says. "You of all people know where I stand with my brother. You and me may not have ended on the best terms, but when we were together, I let you in. And for you to run to him, even as a friend..." He trails off and shakes his head. "It's a betrayal."

"Luke, no, it's not like that," she says. She's already starting to whine, and I am not here for it.

"Then what's it like?" I spit.

She glares at me before her eyes dart to Luke. "You told him he could have me." There's a bit of desperation in her tone. "You called him in front of me and said he was my problem now. You gave both of us permission."

"Because you called me a *fucking loser* when I got home from the playoff game that sent his team to the Super Bowl," Luke says, his voice increasing to a yell before it falls eerily quiet with his next sentence. "You told me you wanted to be with a winner like Jack instead of a *fucking loser* like me."

Whoa.

I knew she called him a loser...but I did *not* know about the part where she called Jack a winner. What a low blow from someone who claims to love him.

Just more examples of how he has surrounded himself with all the wrong people his entire life.

Enter Ellie.

"Why are you even here?" he asks. "Why aren't you bothering him instead of trying to ruin my life?"

"For the baby," she cries.

He blows out a breath. "I'm sorry, Michelle, but I'm married now, and I'm in love with my wife. I will never love you the way I love Ellie."

"But we're having a baby together," she says, actual tears falling down her cheeks now. "Doesn't that mean something to you?"

"Yeah, it does," he says. He stands. "It means I want a paternity test."

Her brows draw together. "You can't be serious."

"Oh, I'm dead serious. And I want my brother's DNA tested against this baby, too." He points at her. "Your refusal to answer my question about whether you've slept together tells me everything I need to know."

"I did," she finally says. "I slept with him after you and I broke up in January. I was so angry with you, and I wanted to hurt you. I wanted to make you jealous."

He shakes his head and snags his bottom lip between his teeth. I'm a silent observer through this entire exchange. "It didn't work. Don't you see that? I'm not jealous that you slept with Jack." He lets out a little chuckle. "I'm disgusted. Get that paternity test done in the next month or you'll hear from my lawyer. If the results show I'm the father, we'll figure something out. Until then, stay on your side of the house. Stay away from my wife and me or find somewhere else to live." He turns to me. "Come on, Ellie, let's go have sex."

My eyes widen at the whirlwind of his monologue, but I stand as instructed and follow my husband up the stairs to our bedroom.

CHAPTER 24

"Are you okay?" I ask tentatively once I shut the door behind me. He collapses on the bed and lies back to stare up at the ceiling.

"Not really," he admits.

I sit on the edge of the bed then lie back beside him. "Wanna talk about it?"

"Not really."

"Do it anyway?" My voice is a hopeful question, and he chuckles. "You'll feel better." I nudge him a little with my elbow.

"It's just a lot, training camp and preseason games and everything, and we're playing the Broncos this week so the added pressure of the team who beat us in the playoffs. And then to have to come home to *that*—to find out my ex slept with my brother, or maybe she's still sleeping with him..." He exhales a long breath. "I've come to terms that I'm the father of that baby...but maybe I'm not."

"It *is* a lot. And you know, your wife is supposed to help you carry those burdens." I glance over at him, and he turns his head to lock eyes with me.

He doesn't say anything as a bit of heat passes between us. It's always there, but never more present than when we're lying on a bed together.

"Thanks, Ellie," he says softly.

I reach down and grab his hand. I squeeze it. I want to ask how he'll feel if it isn't his baby—or how he'll feel if it *is*. Instead, I ask, "How does it make you feel that she and Jack slept together?"

His eyes are still on mine. "I'm disgusted by it, but they're free to do what they want. They deserve each other."

"Does it hurt?" I pry.

"I was done with her over a year ago, but it took me a little time to get up the nerve to actually end it. I don't know how she thought sleeping with my brother would somehow translate to getting me back, but that's Michelle for you. She's fucked up, but my choices are limited given who her father is." He shakes his head and moves his eyes back to the ceiling. "I wish I would've known who she was from the start. I never would've gotten involved with her if I had."

"So what if she gets the test done and we find out the baby isn't yours?"

He's quiet as he mulls that one over. "I don't know," he says. "I know it's not ideal, especially not with her, but there's still a part of me who keeps thinking about the baby. I figured I'd have kids down the road. I'm still young, and maybe family, kids...maybe that's where I want my focus to be eventually." He's edging around talks about *the future* even though it's a known superstition that brings bad luck in his eyes.

He wants kids *someday*...and now he's married to me for a year, which pushes *someday* further back—unless Michelle really is carrying his baby, in which case *someday* might actually just be a few months away.

What a mess.

"And what about Jack's role in all this?" I ask. I flex my fingers in his.

"If anything hurts, it's the betrayal there. But at least I understand his motivation. He has wanted to get me back for everything that happened with Savannah for years, and he thought he found that opportunity when Michelle came knocking. But even so, I can't help wondering how we even got here. How our relationship got so fucked up that his first move is to try to hurt me."

"I only saw him for a minute today, but he told me to warn you about Allen Hammond." I keep my eyes on his profile as I say those words, and Luke winces.

"Not much I can do about him," he says.

"I looked him up," I admit. "He sounds like a real asshole."

He grunts out a laugh. "He is. He's sidelined me for a few plays. He's left me with more than a few bruises. He's as tough as they come, and he's also one of the few really dirty players in the league."

"Because he intentionally hurts people?"

Luke nods. "Nobody wants to *injure* anyone. You can't take away someone's livelihood like that. But *hurting* them? Taking them out for a few plays or even for the rest of the game? There's still a few guys around with that old school way of thinking, and Hammond is one of them."

"So how do you protect yourself?"

He shrugs. "I play the game. I get out there and defend myself the best way I know how. I catch the ball and run it into the end zone."

"How many career touchdowns do you have?"

"Sixty-seven," he says without missing a beat.

"Wow," I say. I'm not sure if that number is impressive or not.

"I'm in the top hundred of all-time career TDs for a single player. I'm actually one TD away from tying a spot in the top fifty."

There's my answer. "Holy shit, Luke. That's impressive."

He chuckles. "Just doing what I love."

"Speaking of *doing what you love*," I say, trailing off.

He chuckles. "Is that an invitation?"

I sit up and then I turn and toss one leg over him so I'm straddling him. I shift my hips over his. "Well you did invite me up here for sex," I point out.

He chuckles. "Yeah, I did do that, didn't I?"

I lean down and press a soft kiss to his lips, and then I sit up over him as I continue to move my hips over his growing erection. "Whatever happens, Luke, I love you. I'm rooting for you, and I don't just mean from the stands. I'm on your side and I'm here."

He reaches up to pull me down so my lips are inches from his. "I love you, too. Thank you for being you. For being so different from all the mistakes of my past."

And then there are no more words as his lips meet mine.

CHAPTER 25

"You can expect the results in seven to ten business days," the tech tells Luke as he places a bandage over a small cotton ball on his arm.

"Any way we can speed that up?" Luke asks.

The tech gives Luke a tight smile. "Not really but you can still try if you're offering to grease my palm."

Luke chuckles. "Understood. Thanks."

We leave the lab, and I let Michelle take the front seat next to Luke since she almost passed out again and claims the backseat makes her carsick.

"I was hoping we'd have the results before I have to leave for Denver," Luke says on our way home. It was a long shot anyway since he leaves in three days.

"Guess we won't," Michelle says, and I sense more than a little bit of smugness in her tone.

Whatever. I roll my eyes behind my sunglasses. She can be smug all she wants. She's the one who forced her way into our home. She's the one sleeping alone in Luke's house while Luke keeps me warm at night.

We're quiet the rest of the way home, each of us lost in our own thoughts, and it's not until after dinner when Michelle heads out with some friends that I find out what he was thinking.

We're sitting on the couch, Pepper in between with her butt against my leg—of course—and her head perched on Luke's leg. He scratches her absently behind the ears and I'm petting a pattern on her back when he glances at me. "Can I talk to you about something?"

My eyes lock on his. "Always."

"This whole mess with Michelle just has me thinking a lot about what I want out of life. You know?" He scratches a trail from Pepper's head down to my hand, where he links his fingers through mine. "Do you want kids?" he asks.

I nod. "Yeah. Someday. Ideally a few years down the road, and I'd love a boy and a girl, sort of like Josh and me. I want them to be close like we are. What about you?"

"I never thought I did, mostly because I didn't want multiple kids who would grow up to turn on each other. But regardless of what happens with the paternity test results, yeah, I do, too. Kids will eventually grow into adults who can make their own decisions. It's the parents' job to give their kids the tools to foster healthy relationships with their siblings."

"How many do you want?" I ask.

"Two sounds good," he says. His fingers tighten in mine, and my eyes fall to where our hands are connected. "Especially if they're with you."

I glance up at him, and he gives me a small smile. I lower my voice just in case Michelle is around to overhear. "What are you saying?"

"I'm saying I want this," he says, using his other hand to wave between the two of us, "to be real. I don't want some stupid contract laying out our future. I don't want either of us to hold any anxiety about what happens when the term is up. In fact..." He trails off and stands, and he leaves the room. He returns a minute later with some papers in his hand, and then he ceremoniously rips them in half.

It's just figurative since I still have my signed copy, but the sentiment is there, and tears spring to my eyes.

"It's you and me, Ellie. I might be a different person during the season, and I want you to just hold out for the me you know. He'll be back, and we'll have our life back in a couple months, and we'll be stronger for it." My mind immediately moves to overdrive. What does he mean that he might be a different person? How, exactly?

I don't get a chance to ask because he keeps talking.

"I just want all this nonsense," he says, shaking our contract, "to be off the table. This Michelle business is making me see how very much I want kids someday. A family. With you."

He sits back down, but this time beside me instead of on the other side of Pepper. He's close, and he murmurs softly when he speaks again.

"I never thought I'd get married again," he says. "I never thought I'd have kids. And then you tumbled into my life at a damn nightclub of all places and somehow you brought me everything I didn't know I was missing. Be my wife, Ellie. For real." He drops a kiss just below my ear on my neck, and I shiver at the feeling.

"You and me," I murmur, and his lips trail over to my mouth.

He kisses me briefly—way too briefly—before he pulls back. "Is that a yes?"

"Oh, hell yes, that's a yes," I say, and then he pushes me back. Pepper jumps off the couch at my sudden movement, but I hardly notice because Luke's mouth is hot on mine, his tongue assaulting mine in the most heavenly way as an ache presses ferociously between my legs.

"Fuck me," I murmur. "Right here. Right now."

He answers by shifting up off me to unbuckle his belt. He fumbles with my jeans before he shoves them down, and I kick off one leg so I have enough room to spread my legs for his lean body. And then he shoves into me without foreplay, and holy hell. My eyes roll back into my head at the perfect feeling of his entrance. He rocks into me right there on the couch, and there's something so simple about having sex with my husband on our couch even though there are so many other complications clouding our relationship.

But those complications don't matter.

We're sealing our new commitment. It's a new promise. It's pure and beautiful with a little magic thrown in, and as he drives in and out of me, he pushes my body to the brink. I collapse over it, freefalling into an orgasm that shifts my world off its axis as the contractions of my body over his sends him into his own climax. He grunts into me. "Oh, fuck, Ellie, yes," he mutters. "Fuck, fuck, fuck." His words punctuate his thrusts as my body milks every ounce of pleasure from his.

It's over far too soon, and as he pulls out of me and shimmies back into his jeans before helping me with mine, something here feels different. It's a renewal of our vows with a lot more meaning behind them this time. It's a promise that we're both in this. We'll both fight for this.

It's real. Him and me. Forever.

CHAPTER 26

Of all the cities in the world for the Aces to have their season opener, of course it would be Denver. That means a risk of running into Jack and also more anxiety over whether this Allen Hammond guy is going to ram into my husband's chest in some asshole move to sideline him.

The stakes are higher this time, and it's palpable as Nicki and I walk into the stadium. We're wearing our specially-made Aces jerseys showcasing our husbands' numbers, and we get a few leers as we walk through another team's home stadium to our seats.

It's the first Sunday of the regular season, and Luke left Friday to travel with the team to Denver...as did Michelle. She doesn't have a key position with the team, but since her dad owns the team, apparently that means she can do whatever she wants.

Nicki and I took the short flight yesterday morning, and we're sharing a suite at the same hotel where the team is staying. We had a quick few minutes with our men last night and again this morning, but otherwise they've been busy with their team responsibilities as they get ready to play a team who handily beat them just two weeks ago.

But they're ready now. They're serious. This one counts. The starters will be in.

And that's why it feels extra ominous when a strange sensation washes over me as we walk toward our seats. I may not know the details of whatever secret Savannah holds over the Dalton brothers, but for some reason, she slithers into my mind.

I ask Nicki out of the blue, "Does Savannah come to these things?"

She shrugs and purses her lips. "Doubtful, but given her history with both brothers, maybe. She'd probably love to run another profile on the two of them, and what better event to dig up dirt than when they're playing each other?"

Speaking of Luke's exes, I bring up the other pain in my ass. "Think we'll be lucky enough to run into Michelle today?"

She laughs. "We'll definitely see her on the sidelines. Maybe after the game, too, if we go to the team dinner. How's that whole living with her thing going, by the way?"

I roll my eyes. "About as awful as you'd expect. But I'm hopeful for good news when the paternity results come in."

"When are those supposed to show up?" She pauses to look at the numbers at the top of each section in the stadium to find the ones that match our tickets.

I stop with her, and we find our section. "With any luck, they'll be waiting for us when we get back home." We both turn in and show our tickets to the attendant at the top of a long row of stairs.

"I've got my fingers crossed for you."

We opted for tickets we found in the third row near the fifty-yard line on the away team's side of the field. My heart thumps when we slide into our seats, and it starts racing when the announcer introduces the Vegas Aces. Nicki and I cheer like a couple of maniacs, drawing the ire of several Broncos fans sitting nearby.

I spot eighty-four right away as he runs beside my brother, and I can't help but stare at his long, lean frame as he rushes across the field from the locker room they just came out of toward the sideline.

God, he's hot. And I'm *married* to him.

This still doesn't feel real. I didn't even know him a few months ago, and somehow we're living out our fairy tale now. He's in love with me. I'm in love with him. We're giving this a real effort.

I'm a nervous wreck as a handful of players move to the center of the field for the coin toss. The Aces will get the ball first, and a bunch of men line up on either side of the ball for kickoff. I say a little prayer in my head. *Please keep him safe. Please don't let him get hurt.*

I look for eighty-four. "Is he out there?" I ask Nicki, and before she answers, I find him standing on the sidelines as he waits for his turn to take the field.

She shakes her head. "The special teams unit goes out there for kickoff. But he'll be on for the next play."

And then the players are running at each other.

"Go, go, go!" Nicki yells as some guy in a black and red uniform runs with the ball. He makes it to the thirty-yard line before he's tackled, and I wince at the contact. God, that can't feel good.

We watch as a bunch of players run off the field, and then I spot Luke as he runs on.

Number three, Brandon Fletcher, hands the ball off to Jaxon Bryant for the first play for no gain. He does that again on the second play, and this time Jaxon gets away and manages to get a first down. I only know this from the announcer narrating the events.

My eyes are zeroed in on number eighty-four. I watch as he fights off Hammond to try to get free, but he seems unable to escape him.

On the next play, Fletcher throws to my brother, who makes a big gain and another first down.

They don't get much further than that, and the first drive is over for the Aces, ending with no score as it's the Broncos turn to take the field.

I breathe out a little sigh of relief that Luke isn't on the field for a while. I can breathe easier while he rests. I sort of like when the other team has the ball just for that very reason, though I'm sure he's itching to get back on the field to try to escape Hammond.

I watch Jack as he goes to work. I don't know him well, but from the few interactions I've had with him, it's safe to say that he's a confident guy. That translates to the field, too.

I watch as the center snaps the ball to him, and all the linemen protect him from the defenders who are trying their hardest to take him down. He's clearly in his element as he takes his time scanning the field, watching his men move into the places where they're supposed to go based on the strategies the team has practiced over and over. The way he stands there before he throws the ball reminds me a lot of the way he acts in his everyday life. He takes his time, he waits with poise, and then he throws the ball with accurate precision.

A wide receiver catches it and gains a few yards before one of the Aces defenders takes him down.

I can't help but picture Thanksgiving at the Dalton house as Carol and Kaylee made the turkey inside and the boys went outside to toss around the ball. I can just see Jack and Luke making even a simple game of catch into a competitive sport.

It actually sort of helps me understand their relationship now in a way. The competitive spirit has always been there between them, starting with sports but not ending there. Clearly that spirit has infiltrated every aspect of their relationship, and I can't help but wonder if it's beyond repair.

They're two stubborn men, and Luke obviously drew the short end of the stick when it comes to fitting in with his own family.

Enter Ellie.

I'm his family now. Josh is. Even my parents are.

I text my mom. I'm sure they're watching the game. In fact, I bet they'll come to Vegas next weekend for the home opener.

Me: *Will you be in Vegas next weekend? Luke and I would love to take you to dinner.*

I'd invite them to stay with us, but we have that whole *Michelle* issue going on.

With any luck, she'll be out of the house by next weekend. Surely we'll get the test results in the next few days, and I'm certain those results will show us that Luke isn't her baby's daddy. And I can't wait. I can't wait to get her out of our house. I can't wait to have Luke to myself. I can't wait to look ahead to our future together—maybe with babies in it, but babies that belong to Luke and me.

The Broncos score, and my chest tightens as some players run off the field while others run on. The Broncos kick the ball back to the Aces, and Jaxon Bryant catches it and runs it all the way to the forty-yard line.

I'm getting pretty good at understanding what's going on.

My eyes zero in on the hottie wearing number eighty-four as he runs into his position. I spot Hammond standing on the line across from him, and something punches me in the gut. I have a sudden bad feeling.

I want Luke off the field.

Maybe it was Jack's ominous threat before the preseason game, or maybe it's just some strange premonition poking at my gut. My stomach twists and I feel like I can't watch as the ball is snapped to Brandon Fletcher.

I watch as Brandon looks around the field for an open receiver. I watch as he spots Luke.

And then I close my eyes as Luke makes the catch.

CHAPTER 27

I regret closing my eyes, but only because in closing them, I heard the crowd's reaction before I saw what actually happened.

The loud cheering and jeering all around me turned to a collective gasp before the entire stadium went silent for a moment.

And it's in that moment of silence that I open my eyes.

I can't see the field because everyone around me is standing. I stand, too, and I see a ring of men surrounding someone on the ground in the spot where Luke caught the ball. I can't see past those men, but I spot Nolan eighteen standing there. Fletcher is nearby, too, as the trainers rush out onto the field. Players from both teams kneel as they wait.

And then Nicki's hand finds mine. She squeezes my hand as we wait with bated breath.

Is he okay?

What just happened?

Should I have kept my eyes open to see? Or will I see it a thousand times over on replay both on television and as it haunts my dreams?

Time seems to slow to a crawl, or maybe it's moving backwards. The stadium remains hushed, but a buzzing in my ears starts to get louder.

And then the big screen replays what just happened.

We watch as Allen Hammond plows into Luke's right knee. It looks like a cheap shot to me, and the bend of Luke's knee looks both unnatural and painful.

I can't watch.

I close my eyes and offer up a little prayer.

Please let him be okay.

Maybe he just got the wind knocked out of him.

"Oh shit," Nicki murmurs beside me.

I see the cart as someone drives it out onto the field, and that sick feeling in my stomach worsens. I may not know much about the game, but I do know that when the cart comes out, it's to clear an injured player off the field so the game can go on.

But how can it go on without Luke?

My heart thumps loudly in my chest. I feel it in my head.

A few players shift out of the way of the cart, and suddenly I can see him just as he sits up with the help of one of the trainers. His helmet is still on, so I can't see his face to get any sort of gauge on how he's doing.

The trainers help him stand. It's hard to see around them, but his knee doesn't look right. I try to suck in deep breaths, but they won't come. My chest feels heavy as I imagine what he's going through right now. His worst fears are being realized. He has an injury that could take him out for the rest of this season, and since he's in the last year of his contract and he's thirty-one and he could need time for rehab, this could be more than just *season*-ending.

And it's happening in Denver. His brother's homefield.

"What do I do?" I cry to Nicki.

"The tunnel," she says. "Let's go find the tunnel. We'll get you down to him."

I nod. I don't know what the tunnel is, but I follow her as we walk down the three rows to the security guard standing on the field near us. "She's his wife," Nicki says, her tone panicked. "Luke Dalton's wife. How do we get to the tunnel?"

The guard looks at her like she's crazy, and then, thankfully, Josh spots us. He rushes over and says something to the guard, and then he lets me onto the field and ushers me toward the tunnel.

Nicki stays behind.

I'm terrified to do this by myself. I don't know where I'm going, and I have no idea what I'm walking into.

Security passes me off to another security guard, who leads me through the back tunnels of the stadium toward the room where Luke is being examined.

This guard knocks on the door, and when we're called in, I spot Luke sitting on an exam table holding a towel pressed to his eyes, his shoulders trembling beneath all that gear. His helmet is off. A team doctor in an Aces polo shirt is typing on a tablet. Luke's injured right leg is stretched out on the table and the left hangs off the side. He's swinging that leg a little in what seems to be a nervous tick.

His tight football pants are pulled up over his knee, which looks like it just got through a warzone. It's already starting to swell, and it just doesn't look right. It doesn't look healthy.

"His wife is here," the guard says, and Luke lowers the towel. His eyes are red and watery, and he's sweaty, and despite all that, a wave of emotion washes over me. Tears spring to my eyes at how damn much I love him.

He's crying, and I can't help but wonder if it's because of the pain or if it's because he knows it's the end of the season and maybe more than that.

I force my own tears away and I stop myself from rushing to his side. I take it slow here. I don't know exactly what he wants from me. Yes, I'm his wife. Yes, we're in love. Yes, we're giving this a real try. But the reality is that we're still getting to know each other.

This is the moment where I need to be strong for my husband—where I need to show him what I'm made of as his *wife*. I offer a smile. "Hey good lookin'," I say. "You come here often?"

He doesn't smile, but a slight tick of his neck calls me to his side.

"Can you help me out of this?" he asks, tugging at his jersey. His voice is soft as he fights off his emotions.

"Of course," I murmur. I tug at it. It's on there tight. I wrestle with it and can't even imagine how he actually got it on. "Dammit," I mutter. "Is there a lock on this thing? Why's it so tight?"

"So defenders can't grab it." His voice isn't just soft. It's hollow and flat. It's missing the element of *him*.

I finally wrestle it off and help with his shoulder pads, and then I reach over and hug his head to my chest. He wraps an arm around my arms, and this big, strong man quivers beneath the hold I have on him as he allows some of his very big emotions out. "What's the word, Doctor?" I ask the man examining Luke, my voice soft and soothing as I hold Luke to me.

"We've got a dislocated knee and possible torn ACL, but we won't get the full picture until we get an MRI," the doctor tells me. "We've got an ambulance on the way now. If it was a kneecap, that's simple, but this is a total knee dislocation, and that requires emergency treatment."

"How long is the recovery on a dislocation?" I ask.

"Nine to twelve months depending whether there's any nerve damage. If we're also dealing with a torn ACL as I suspect, it could be even longer."

Luke lets out a small yelp of protest as he continues to shudder beneath me.

"Does it hurt?" I ask softly.

"Like a motherfucker." His words come through gritted teeth.

"What can I do?" I ask.

"Nothing," he mutters.

He lets go of his grip on my arms as he seems to draw into himself at the mention of potentially being out for a year or even longer.

This injury transcends whatever bullshit he has going on with Michelle and his boss. It's bigger than our "fake" marriage.

A year out of the game at this point in his career could very likely mean the end of it. Not only will he need time to heal and get healthy, but when he returns, he'll be another year older. He may not have the same range of motion with a bum knee. He'll be another year less agile. He'll have another year on the kids joining the team right out of college, which in football is detrimental.

He's scared. I get that. But my job is to be here for him. To be the place he leans while we work together to pick up the pieces and figure out the recovery plan so he can get back to doing what he loves.

Instead, he's already pushing me away. I feel it.

And I don't know what to do.

CHAPTER 28

I ride in the ambulance with him. I clutch his hand in mine. I mutter nonsense about how everything's going to be okay. I don't know if it'll be okay. We don't know the full extent of his injury yet, and I certainly don't know how he's going to deal with it—emotionally or physically. I don't know what it means for him...for us.

"What's the score?" he asks.

I chuckle. I can't help but think it's *so him* to want to make sure his teammates are okay as he's on his way to the hospital to assess whether he'll be out nine months or forever. I pull my phone out of my pocket and see about a million missed messages and calls. I'll get to them when I get to them.

I search for the score. "The Aces have the lead. Seventeen to ten at halftime."

He doesn't react, and I hate how he's a total blank slate. He's always been private, and he's always done a pretty good job of hiding how he's really feeling, but it's okay to smile when your team is winning. Unless, I guess, you're the injured player on the way to the hospital who can't contribute to that win. The one who can't celebrate that win.

Tears pinch behind my eyes again.

When we get to the hospital, we're checked in through the emergency room. I sit and wait on a chair in a little room with a curtain while he's carted off for his MRI. It's only then I pull out my phone and check my messages.

I see Nicki's first.

Nicki: *What's going on? Is he okay?*

Me: *He's okay. We just got to the hospital. We'll know more after the MRI.*

I check the ones from my mom next.

Mom: *We'd love to visit with you two.*

Mom: *We just saw the hit. Is he okay? It looks bad.*

I don't have the energy to come up with something new to tell her, so I just copy the same message I sent to Nicki. Those are the only people in my circle who really need to know what's going on.

I'm so new at this that I don't even know my place yet. I assume I shouldn't talk to the press...yet I'm more than his wife. I'm his publicist, and handling the press is sort of my job when it comes to him.

I think of all the times Luke had ESPN on to catch the highlights. Any time someone was hurt in virtually any sport, it was the coach's press conference where we learned more. Either there was no new information or the coach gave some indication of how severe the injury is.

Luke returns from the MRI. He puts the game on the television as we wait on the results. He's silent as he stares blankly at the screen.

The doctor comes in with a clipboard a while later. "The good news is that it doesn't look like there's any nerve damage," he begins. "The bad news is that you're going to need an open reduction to reset the bone."

"What's open reduction?" Luke grunts.

"When you have a dislocated knee, there are two ways to put it back into place. Closed reduction means without surgery where we do what we can to shift it back into place. Open reduction means surgery. You've also torn your ACL, which will require surgery as well. I can get you scheduled for surgery this week or you can go home and have it done there."

"I'd like to go home so our team doctors can give me a second opinion."

"Of course," the doctor says. "I understand. But it's a cut and dry injury, Mr. Dalton. I guarantee you'll hear the same answer from your doctors back home."

"Still," Luke says.

The doctor nods. "I assume your team heads home tomorrow?"

Luke nods.

"We'll fit you for a knee brace and crutches so you can travel back with them. No weight whatsoever on your knee until you check in with your doctors back home. Don't let it go untreated for too long or you risk nerve damage."

"Thanks," Luke mutters. I grab his hand as the doctor walks out.

"You sure you want to go home instead of just getting the surgery done as soon as possible?" I ask.

"They'll have me cut open Monday night and I'll be back home by Wednesday," he says. He doesn't look at me as he says it. Instead, his eyes are back on the television screen. The news is on now. The game is over, and we're watching a story about one of the highways here in Denver.

I don't even know what to say to that. I'd rather see him just get it done instead of risking it by going home with the team, but I get him wanting to be back home for it. He trusts the team doctors—after all, they've been his doctors for nearly the last decade.

The curtain opens, and a head appears there. "Can I come in?"

Luke glances at the doorway, and then he shuts off the television as he stares across the small space at his brother.

"What are you doing here?" he asks.

"Came to check on my little brother." Jack steps fully into the room and slides the curtain closed. "You okay?"

I don't know why seeing him here makes the heat press behind my eyes again. Maybe it took this terrible turn of events for Luke to smooth things over with his family. Or maybe not. I don't even know if that's something he wants.

"Dislocated knee and torn ACL," Luke says flatly.

"Fuck," Jack mutters. "Not again."

Luke blows out a breath. "Yeah. Again." His eyes turn red as he fights to keep his emotions away, and then he bites his lip.

"I was kidding when I threatened you with Hammond. I had no idea he'd really take a dirty hit on you. He'll get a fine," Jack says. He walks to the foot of the bed.

"He'll get a fine and I'm out for the season. My entire career might be over. But at least he'll get a fine." Luke presses his palms to his eyes, and I'm shocked he's showing such vulnerability in front of his brother.

"It'll be okay, Luke," Jack says softly. Soothingly. In a tone I've never heard out of him before, least of all when it comes to his brother. "Better your knee than your neck, right?"

"It's over either way."

"Come on, man," Jack says, gripping the foot of the bed with both hands. I can't help but wonder if he's thinking he may not have too many years left, either. "Don't be so dramatic. You've got your life. You've got a woman who loves you. Life will move on whether or not you get to play again, and you got nine solid years out of the league. That's way more than most. You and I both know NFL stands for Not For Long."

Luke sniffs in response, and I squeeze his hand. "He's right that you've got a woman who loves you," I say. "I'm right here, whatever you need. Through all of this." My tone is fierce.

"You just can't let what happened the last time you tore your ACL happen again," Jack says, still gripping the footboard.

"What happened the last time?" I ask.

The brothers lock eyes for a beat, and some silent communication passes between them before they both turn their eyes back to me.

Jack's expression is riddled with something resembling guilt. Maybe it's guilt for letting something slip just now in front of me...or maybe it's more. I get the feeling it's more. Much, much more.

Something so big that it severed his relationship with Luke. Yet he showed up here again.

He still cares about his brother.

Or maybe he's here as a warning. Maybe he's here to remind his brother not to let whatever happened last time happen again.

What the hell happened?

"Nothing," Jack murmurs. "I, uh, just meant the recovery time." I've never heard this man stutter over his words before. Not once. This is the self-assured, confident man who both speaks and acts with precision and care. Always.

He's lying. Something happened between these brothers the last time Luke tore his ACL, and it was enough to force a wedge between the two of them and between Luke and the rest of his family.

And I'm going to figure out the truth. No matter what it takes, I will fight for Luke.

I have to. He's not just my "husband." He's the man I plan on spending the rest of my life with.

And there's this one other thing.

As I was sitting in the room waiting for Luke to return from his MRI, I realized something as I glanced through my calendar trying to piece together how to handle his injury with the media.

My period is late.

To be concluded in Book 5, **END GAME.**

ACKNOWLEDGMENTS

Thank you to my husband for everything you do. The support, encouragement, and love is what makes this possible. Thank you to my kids for nap time and quiet time when mommy gets to write, and thank you to my parents who love hanging out with my babies so I can get some computer time in.

Thank you to Trenda London from It's Your Story Content Editing, Diane Holtry and Alissa Riker for beta reading, Najla Qamber for the gorgeous cover design, and Katie Harder-Schauer from Proofreading by Katie.

Thank you to Wildfire Marketing, my ARC team, Team LS, and all the bloggers who read, post, and review.

Thank you to you, the reader, for taking time out of your life to spend it with Ellie. I hope you enjoyed what you read, and I can't wait for you to read the final book.

ABOUT THE AUTHOR

Lisa Suzanne is a romance author who resides in Arizona with her husband and two kids. She's a former high school English teacher and college composition instructor. When she's not cuddling or chasing her kids, she can be found working on her latest book or watching reruns of *Friends*.

ALSO BY LISA SUZANNE

A LITTLE LIKE DESTINY
A Little Like Destiny Book One
#1 Bestselling Rock Star Romance

TAKE MY HEART
My Favorite Band Book One
#1 Bestselling Rock Star Romance